I0547211

Diary of a Madwoman

and Other Stories

Edited by

JULIA T. LYE

DeeBee

Diary of a Madwoman and Other Stories

Copyright © 2020 by DeeBee Books

All rights reserved. Printed in the United States of America. No part of this book may be used or reproduced in any manner whatsoever without written permission from the individual author and publisher except in the case of brief quotations embodied in critical articles or reviews. Individual authors retain all copyrights. This book is a work of fiction. Names, characters, businesses, organizations, places, events and incidents either are the product of the authors' imaginations or are used fictitiously. Any resemblance to actual persons, living or dead, events, or locales is entirely coincidental.

For information contact David Allan Hamilton:

davidallanhamilton00@gmail.com

www.deebeebooks.com

Layout by Léa Marshall-Raymond

Cover art by Irina Vorotyntseva

ISBN: 9781896794365

First Edition: June 2020

10 9 8 7 6 5 4 3 2 1

CONTENTS

Aegis

By Jonathan Kao

ALIEN.

What do you think of when someone mentions the word alien? Maybe wide-eyed monsters who plan on taking the world into their grasps. Maybe flying UFOs in their circular shape, which is funny, because anything could be an unidentified flying object if it could fly and if one person couldn't recognize it. Or maybe even an alien superhero, such as Superman or Martian Manhunter. The meaning of aliens has changed quite a lot over the years, and most people don't even know the real, true meaning. Google states that the word alien means belonging from a foreign country or region. And that's the thing. Those aliens, that you imagine, aren't aliens. They don't come from a different world. In reality, they're from ours. You heard me right. The aliens that you all know and love are from Earth. Or at least, the aliens in this story.

Those aliens were born on Earth, but a different time than us, when fire and starvation were the only things that they knew. They originated way back during the age of dinosaurs or, more specifically, their death, when the comet hit the Earth and smoke covered the entire planet. The aliens grew up in caves, or underground, as that was really the only way to survive the crisis outside. But, like all things, that time passed. And in its place was a time of peace. In that time, the aliens evolved and learned to create objects and tools. The aliens were the first intelligent people on Earth. And they lived peacefully for a long time, for about 66 million years. And then, the humans arrived.

One thing you should know is that the aliens knew that peace was the answer. They knew that fighting over things as simple as land was a complete waste of time. And that included humans. The aliens couldn't waste their time on small things like that. So they built Aegis. Aegis was supposed to be a last resort. A last resort to destroy humans. After all, the aliens were advanced, and the humans weren't. Except, the aliens couldn't use it. The humans took Aegis, and drew the aliens off Earth, to a new planet, called Torpaq.

And they've been there ever since, waiting for the perfect time to reclaim what was once theirs.

*

"DODGE THE BALL!" I heard a voice shout beside me.

A red foam ball flew straight at my face, spinning way too quickly to be going straight. It was getting bigger. Wait, no. It was getting closer.

"Duck!" a girl's voice said.

It was gym class. And I was the last one on my team. Again. It didn't exactly help that I stood in the corner most of the time, but being last still sucked. It meant that my entire team was rooting for me. Which put a lot of pressure on a guy like me. And if I lost, they would pretty much ban me from being on their team again. Even though we didn't choose teams.

The red ball was now close enough that I could see the small holes made by students who, I guess, needed a giant stress ball. Not that this was surprising. The students who went to school here definitely needed some stress relievers.

I quickly sidestepped the ball at the last second. There were whoops from the sidelines. I would say only my team's bench, but everyone on the other team had gotten revived, while my team was all crowded on the same bench.

There was an unusual silence from the other side. The entire team was huddled together in a circle, discussing something. What were they doing?

I picked up the red ball and threw it at them. Too bad my throwing skills weren't on par with my dodging skills. The ball rolled harmlessly away on the other side of the basketball court.

I glanced at my team. They were all confused too. Not just everyone stopped the battle to talk about a strategy. In fact, no one in my school did. Or from another school, for that matter.

The other team suddenly dispersed. They went around picking up the balls on the floor and in the corners. Then, they all stood in a line, each one holding a ball at the ready.

Oh crap, I thought. There was only one explanation for this type of behavior. They were going to throw all of the balls at once.

Or, maybe, they were going to politely throw one at a time.

Yeah, I didn't think so.

"3… 2… 1… FIRE!" one of the guys on the other team shouted. The entire team threw their dodgeballs at me.

I had a split second to think. I picked up a ball on the floor and raised it to a ball that was heading my way. *Splunk!* The ball bounced off of mine and bounced harmlessly to the ground. Surprisingly, there weren't any other balls that even came near me. Luck? Or maybe the Force? OR, maybe even the requirements of the plot?

I looked up. The other team was getting ready for round two. Jeez. How many balls did the school have? There were like thirty people on the other side with seconds, plus some of the balls that were already on my side before the big ball massacre. That's like… um, a lot of dodgeballs!

Kidding. I know how to do math. Thirty times two is easily fifty. Oh, you caught me. Just making sure you were paying attention.

"FIRE!" the same guy shouted. The team threw all of the balls they had at me. Only, there weren't as many because they had used up most of them. Unfortunately, all of the good throwers still had the balls. Which meant I had to move, since I didn't have a dodgeball to protect myself.

I examined the incoming fire. There was a space that had no balls incoming. I could easily sidestep to that spot and live for another round.

My teammates must have seen it too because they were desperately trying to tell me to go over there.

Only, I couldn't. My legs were frozen. I couldn't move. *Not now! Come on! Why couldn't I have nervous breakdowns during art class?*

"Move it!" a girl shouted at me. Gee, what did she think I was trying to do? Yeah, I'll just stand here with a cup of tea and do nothing as large balls were being thrown at my face! Did you read that in a British accent and then abruptly change to an angry Canadian? Good, that's what I was going for.

"Shut up!" I yelled to my teammates, without looking at them. Which sort of gave the impression that I was shouting at a dodgeball. I wasn't, for the record.

I tried one last time to move to the no-hit zone, but without luck. What happened to that awesome plot save in round one? Has the author already lost hope in me?

Even if the author has lost hope in the epic main character, I still needed to dodge this stupid ball.

And that stupid ball was closing in on me. *Move you idiot!* I yelled to myself, but it didn't work. I was still stuck to the ground.

"Ouch!" I said as the, ahem, foam ball smacked my face. Admittedly, the ball didn't hurt that much, since it was a foam ball.

"NOOOOOO!" my teammates shouted at me. Relax, it's just a game. It's not like aliens with energy blasters were attacking me, was it? (Foreshadowing.)

"That took longer than expected," Mr. Alienable, my gym teacher, said. *Alienable?* You ask in disbelief. Yeah, that's his real name. Did you know that alienable means transferable to a new owner? Which is funny 'cause this guy's been married to three different ladies. Plus, his name's got alien in it, so that's also pretty funny.

Mr. Alienable got up from where he was relaxing on the sidelines with a hot cup of joe and walked to the middle of the court. "You just lost me some money, kid," he said, pointing at me. "You usually get out at the beginning."

"Um… thanks?" I half asked and half-said.

"It ain't no compliment boy."

So, it was a compliment? Or it wasn't? I could never understand this creature.

"Go get changed. Y'all smell like a sewer rat," Mr. Alienable barked at us.

We all walked to the change rooms. I held my head down in shame. Actually, I was trying to hide from my teammates.

It didn't work. Probably because I was the only one doing it.

"Dude. Why didn't you move?" asked someone. Everyone was crowded around me, sort of like the way reporters surround a criminal. Distancing, and a little annoyance at how horrible that person is.

I shrugged.

"You could have caught the ball. Why didn't you just-"

"Go away Stuart," said a beautiful, angelic voice. I turned around. It was, of course, Chelsea. My best friend and also, sort of, crush. She also tended to hurt people if they didn't listen to her. She played soccer and had a mean kick to the shins. Not that they didn't usually listen to her. She was so perfect that pretty much no one wanted to get on her bad side.

"Hey, Alex," she said to me, making everyone within ear-range look at us.

My name's Alex, in case you were wondering.

"Hi Chelsea," I responded.

"Nice going with the freezing," she grinned at me. It didn't bother me; we teased each other all the time.

"You saw that?" I asked, suddenly self-conscious, despite everything I just said. Even though we teased each other a lot, it didn't ever change the fact that she was the prettiest person in the school / city / state / country / continent / world / solar / system / universe / multi-verse.

"Who didn't? It was like a bombing. Meant for one person," she smirked.

"Okay, well, that's a weird analogy, and besides, only one of them hit me," I tilted my head at her.

We had reached the change rooms by now and I walked in. Chelsea waited outside for me since she technically wasn't in PE right now.

I changed into my normal clothes and headed back out. Chelsea was busy talking to Mr. Alienable. I was pretty sure he had a crush on her, but that would be extremely wrong, so I didn't think about it too much.

I walked up to them and tapped Chelsea on the shoulder. "You ready?" I asked her.

"You bet!" Chelsea said a little too enthusiastically. Mr. Alienable got a weird, sad look in his eye.

"Bye Mr. Alienable," Chelsea said, waving to him. Then she leaned in close and whispered to me. "Oh, thank God you came to rescue me. He was talking about dinner plans."

"I don't know if I should say you're welcome, or if God should," I said.

She grinned at me. "Thank you, my knight in shining armor."

I grinned, knowing it was a joke, but still blushed like crazy.

The bell rang and we both walked out the doors of the gym. I headed to my locker and Chelsea followed me.

"Why are you following me?" I asked her.

"I didn't bring my stuff today. I had a presentation," she said. "Which is the same thing I told you this morning."

"Um, yeah. Yes, you did." I quickly hid my face in my locker to block my super red face. I grabbed my stuff and closed the locker door; my face back to a normal color.

"Your face is red," Chelsea laughed.

Or not.

We walked to the school doors silently. I had a feeling that I was forgetting something, but I couldn't place my finger on what.

We reached the doors and said our goodbyes. Chelsea took the bus, and I had to walk home.

I started the walk alone, like always. I passed by the parking lot of the school, the pizza shop, and the glowing warehouse.

Wait. Glowing warehouse? That couldn't be right.

The warehouse was an abandoned one that I passed by every day. I think I would notice if it was glowing.

Yet, it was glowing. There was no doubt about that. In fact, it was so bright that I had to look away. I looked around. There was no one near. I had two options. Go into the warehouse and investigate the glowing thing, or act like it never happened.

The glowing started to get brighter and brighter. There was no way I was going to pass up a chance like this. Chelsea would never forgive me.

I walked into the warehouse. There was a giant open door that apparently had no lock. I walked into the first room. It was so dark and everything was just black.

I walked into the next room. This one was interesting. There was more black. But there was also a bright light. It was coming from an open doorway. I could just go in.

So, I did. In all of the blackness, there was a single, golden earpiece in the middle of the room.

The golden earpiece looked so inviting. It shined in an unnatural way. And it… glowed. There wasn't any light coming from it, but the area around it was a bright yellow. I picked it up. Nothing happened. The shine was still there, and it seemed to be far brighter than before.

I almost heard a whisper coming from it. Maybe it was playing music like any normal earpiece. I held the earpiece closer to my ear. There was a faint humming. *It was just a normal earpiece, and it was just playing music,* I told myself multiple times. It wasn't working. This had to be magical or something. I mean, come on! It was glowing! I could never just walk away from this.

I had an idea. I would just stick it in my ear to prove that it was normal. Then I would leave and get on that history homework which was due tomorrow.

So, I stuck the thing in my ear, despite the obvious lack of hygiene.

Suddenly, my vision became yellow, and there was a metallic clang.

"What the-" I started. I was interrupted by a voice in my head.

I am Aegis, it said. It was oddly feminine and had a slight British accent.

"Who are you?" I asked. "Where am I?"

I am the living conscience of Aegis. And you are in the same place as you were before activating Aegis, the voice said.

My vision was clearing up. Everything was the same, except it wasn't. Everything in the warehouse was brighter and easier to see. I could tell what all of the tiny things in the room were. A random black object in the corner was now a well-defined duffel bag. I could see every tiny piece of mould. I could hear every tiny little noise. All of my senses were sharpened. It was like I had taken a giant pill, or maybe eaten a giant carrot.

"Do you live in an earpiece?" I asked her.

No, but Aegis does.

"Okay…" I squinted. That made total sense. I rolled my eyes and caught sight of a flash of gold. I looked down at my body and gasped.

"Aegis. What am I wearing?" I asked, trying to say "Aegis" right. I was in a suit of armor. But like video game armor. Like futuristic video game armor.

You are wearing the default suit for an Aegis host. An image appeared in my peripheral vision. It looked almost fake. *A black bodysuit, white patches of armor, and a gold trimming for fun. And of course, the white and gold helmet.*

"I'm wearing that?" I asked. "I look good."

Yes, you are wearing it.

I looked at my white plated hands and grinned. Out of the corner of my eye, I saw a brown leg.

"Holy crap!" I exclaimed, pointing at a giant spider. It was huge; I had no idea how I didn't see it on my way in. I guess with my heightened senses I could see things bigger?

Suddenly, my pointed finger became extremely heavy. It started to droop and fell to rest at my side.

"Aegis," I said, still trying to pronounce it the right way. "What was that?"

It's a tarantula. It's a type of spider, Aegis stated, somewhat sarcastically.

"No! That thing that happened when I pointed!"

That is an attacking method. When thrusting your hand, it will increase the weight of your hand. It takes a while to get used to.

I did an air punch. A sudden rush of weight moved to my fist and I spun around, sort of like when a baseball player whiffs on a pitch.

"Wow. What else can this suit do?" I asked.

A video popped up. Then another. And another. They were all showing special moves that I could do. It was kind of like a video game tutorial. On my far right, I could see the suit materialize an energy shield out of nowhere. Next to that, there was a chain lightning thing where there was a bolt of electricity that jumped to every opponent. Next to that was a sort of dash attack where I rushed into the enemy. Everything was so awesome, except something was out of place. Something was wrong. I had it on the tip of my mind, but I just couldn't get it.

"The humans!" I exclaimed, victorious. "Why is the suit attacking humans?"

Every single video showed a human being attacked and injured. The chain lightning was stunning *humans*. The dash attack was harming *humans*. Even the shield ability was deflecting bullets back at the *humans*.

Do not worry. No actual humans were harmed during this presentation.

"Oh. Good," I said, relief washing over me.

However, those are test subjects designed to look like humans.

"What?" I exclaimed. "Test subjects?"

Well, as your kind says, aliens. Well, technically, they are natives. Your kind, humans, are the metaphorical aliens.

"What? Our kind?" I tried to run my hands through my hair, but my hands just banged uselessly on the helmet. "Are you saying that we're aliens?"

Well, yes, in a metaphorical sense.

"What are you talking about?"

So called aliens used to live on Earth.

"What! Holy crap! Aliens are actually real?" I exclaimed, excited.

Well, in a metaphorical sense, anybody...

"Not in a metaphorical sense!" I yelled, interrupting her. "I mean aliens in movies. Are they real?"

Well, yes.

"What about UFOs? Do they drive those?" I asked excitedly. Forget the awesome suit with powers, aliens were real!

Well, in a metaphorical sense, no. They do identify their space crafts. The most common name among their spacecrafts is 1X09.

"Okay... what do the aliens look like?"

Once again, not aliens.

"Well, to me they are. So, can you just call them aliens?"

Very well.

An image appeared in the visor. I would prefer not to show it to anyone. They looked horrifying, like Voldemort but uglier. They weren't cute green Martians, but instead bear-like animals that wore gold armor.

"That's gross." I grimaced. "Hold on. How do you know so much about these aliens, anyway?" I asked Aegis suspiciously.

Quite simple. I was created by them.

"Hold on! You were created by them?" I asked, gesturing to the image on my visor, but my hand ended up pointing to a garbage can.

If as in them, you mean aliens, then yes.

"So, I'm wearing a suit made from aliens... Awesome!" I shouted, pumping both hands in the air.

A crackle of thunder and a flash of light erupted as I pumped my hands in the air, which made me put them both down very quickly.

"Aegis, what was that?" I asked, kind of scared.

Lightning taunt. Meant to taunt enemies or blind them.

"Oh, cool. But not really. Is there a way to stop randomly deploying abilities? It's annoying."

There is a voice command option.

"Yes, I want that," I said. I started to grin. "I think it's time for the training montage in every hero movie."

I am unaware of what that means, but I suppose I could teach you some of the functions.

"You bet!"

I walked around a bit until I found a large open space with some targets. And by targets, I meant some boxes. "Here is the perfect place!" I shouted.

I suppose, but I think we should make it harder.

An army of aliens appeared out of nowhere.

"Holy-"

Don't worry. They are but projections of the visor. They aren't real.

"Oh, good."

However, I am real and have access to your brain, so if you get hit, I will cause a simultaneous shock that will most likely put you in a hospital.

"Hehe. Good joke," I said, fearful for my life.

Thank you. Oh, thank God. *However, it was not a joke.*

The army of aliens started to march towards me. "Um, Aegis?"

Go ahead.

"Um, oh man. Uh… Lightning Taunt!" I shouted. I raised my arms and there was a flash of light. All of the aliens stopped walking and covered their eyes.

"All, right! That chain lightning move thing!" I raised my hand, just like in the video, and lightning jumped out of it. It jumped to around ten of the aliens, stunning them, but there were still so many left.

One of them chucked a metal spear at me. "Shield! Aegis, shield!!!" I shouted. I raised my hand and a blue energy shield appeared out of nowhere. I raised it to my head, blocking the spear.

This was kind of fun. Besides the threat of Aegis shocking me. That part wasn't fun at all.

Another spear was headed for my face.

I quickly sidestepped it and yelled, "Dash!"

The suit suddenly rushed into the aliens with a flash of golden light and toppled a good number of them. The suit quickly dashed back to the spot where I was just at before activating the ability, evading another spear that would have killed me. The good news was that around half of the aliens were down. The bad news was that I probably had whiplash from traveling too quickly.

"Aegis!" I shouted while trying to dodge spears. "I don't know any other moves!"

Suddenly a sword appeared in my hand. It had a golden hilt and words that read "Athena".

I raised the sword in the air and yelled, trying to act intimidating. Instead, there was a rush of weight to my hand and I dropped the sword.
Might I ask? What was that?

"I don't know, Aegis. It was supposed to be cool," I said, picking up the sword again. "Can you turn off that rush of weight?"
It's called Titanium Fist. But if you don't want it, I can disable it.

"Yes, please!" I said rushing towards the aliens. I swung my sword at the first one. There was a clang as metal hit alien armor, and my sword flew out of my hand and hit against the wall.

"Aegis?" I asked, ducking under a punch thrown by the alien.
The weight of your swings isn't strong enough to harm an alien's skin. That's what Titanium Fist was for. And why it was a default setting.

"Oh, come on! You know what? Just turn it back on!" I yelled, barely avoiding another swing at my chest.
Titanium Fist is reactivated.

I dived to the side of the alien and grabbed my sword. "Okay. Let's do this," I muttered to myself, getting into position. A crowd of aliens surrounded me.

"HI-YA!" I exclaimed, swinging my sword at all of them. They all disintegrated into bubbles.

I sat down on the concrete floor of the warehouse. I had done it. I had defeated an entire army of aliens. And I felt great. I wasn't tired or sore or...

The suit gives you an alien medication. Sort of like painkillers, except 1.8 quintuple times better than that, Aegis said, somehow reading my mind.

"Better than that? Shouldn't I be passed out by now?" I asked. "Because of my fragile human body?"

1.8 quintuple times better than pain killing. Not the passing out part. Also, these were all just a figment of the visor, so you can't really be hurt.

"Even if it was a figment of the visor," I said, quoting Aegis. "Wasn't that insane? I had no idea I was that good at fighting!"

You aren't. The suit was fighting for you.

Oh. That made a little more sense. There was no way I was able to fight that good. And definitely no way that I could keep that calm during a real battle. I mean, technically, it wasn't real, but it felt real. And there was the threat of being shocked by Aegis.

I'd say this was extremely successful. This suit was the best thing that happened to me since... ever.

"Hello? Is someone in there?" a very familiar voice shouted from outside the warehouse.

I recognized that voice. I knew it from somewhere, I just couldn't place where. It was feminine and had a light ring to it that made her sound dorky but beautiful.

"Hello? I heard a loud clang. Is someone else here?" the voice said again.

Wait. I knew that voice.

Chelsea?

I stood up. What was Chelsea doing here? I started to walk over to the exit.

What are you doing? Aegis must be kept a secret.

"Are you kidding? Chelsea's my best friend." *And this might impress her,* I thought.

I reached for the door and suddenly heard a scream from Chelsea.

"Chelsea!" I yelled. I rushed through the door and may or may not have broken it. I grimaced. It was a metal door. Jeez, how did I do that?

But that didn't matter. Chelsea was in danger. She wasn't just in danger; she was in the air? In the arms of an... alien? At least, it looked like one. And I should know; I fought an entire fake army of them.

"Aegis? Can this thing fly?" I yelled, running to try to catch up with the alien and Chelsea.

No. But, it can jump extremely high.

"Yeah, let's do that," I said in between sharp breaths.

I planted my foot hard into the ground and propelled myself upwards. I glanced down. I was super far up. I could barely see anything!

In a matter of moments, I was right behind the alien and Chelsea.

Then, everything happened so quickly. The alien turned and grimaced at me. Chelsea was in shock and her beautiful face was scrunched up in confusion. My arm turned into a blaster and fired a small disc at the alien. Aegis was talking about physics that was way too complicated for me.

And I started to fall.

The wind rushed past me and the alien began to get smaller and smaller.

"Aegis!" I shouted, staring at the ground that was getting bigger every second.

Open your arms quickly and brace for impact.

"Brace for impact?" Aegis may be smart, but even with an alien suit, my brain would ram into my skull and I would die. And this suit had to be able to do something. There was no way I was just going to brace for impact and die.

"Aegis! I'm not just going to give up!" I shouted over the loud winds. "Chelsea needs my help!"

Open your arms.

"Aegis! There has to be something this suit can do!" I could see the tiny cracks in the ground by now.

I said, open your arms!

There was nothing to lose. The ground was a couple of feet away.

I closed my eyes and opened my arms. I braced for the moment of pain that I would experience before death. At least I got to see Chelsea one last time.

Nothing happened.

I opened my eyes slowly. The ground was a foot below me. And I was flying. No, wait. Correction. I was gliding. But it felt like flying, even though I was so close to the ground. It was majestic and...

"Ouch!" I said as my face hit the ground.

You do realize you don't glide forever, Aegis stated. I couldn't tell, but it sounded like she was snickering at me.

"Shut up," I said to Aegis, groaning as I stood up. Where were the alien painkillers now?

"We need to get Chelsea," I said. She needed my help. "What was that about? I thought aliens were good?"

What makes you say that?

"They created you. Right?"

Yes, they created me. As a weapon.

"Hold on. What do you mean? A weapon?"

Aegis was a weapon meant to exterminate the human race.

"Whoa!" I exclaimed, my heart racing. "You're a weapon?"

Did the swords not give it away?

Aegis was meant to destroy the human race? That made no sense. Why was she helping me then? Wouldn't she be actively trying to kill me or something?

"Okay," I said, breathing slowly. "You were meant to destroy the human race?"

Yes.

"Then why isn't the human race, you know, destroyed?"

Humans took me. And whoever wears me is who makes the decision.

Whoever wears her. That's not weird at all.

"So as long as you don't get into the wrong hands, you won't demolish us humans?"

No.

I exhaled, feeling much better. "Good."

So back to training? Another army of aliens appeared in front of me. Only this time, they had energy weapons and not metal. And their armor was brighter in the sun.

"No!" I shouted. The aliens disappeared. "We have to save Chelsea!"

Which we cannot do unless you train.

"We need to save Chelsea," I said through gritted teeth.

Very well.

"Okay. How are we going to get her?" I asked. "We have no idea where she's going."

Actually, we do.

"You know I love it when you talk like that. Except, you know, I hate it."

I can tell.

"Good, but enough of this. You said you know how to find Chelsea?" I asked.

Yes. As you already know, I put a tracker on the alien.

So that's what that small disc was.

"Okay. Where are they headed?"

Looks like they're headed to the downtown area.

"Okay. The baddies always do. We need to get there," I said confidently. "Um… How do we get there?"

Unfortunately, none of the abilities associated with Aegis allows fast travel over a long distance.

"So, there's no way to get to Chelsea?" I asked, worried.

I didn't say that.

*

"WHY COULDN'T THE ALIENS JUST MAKE A JETPACK OR SOMETHING?"

Are the other abilities not enough?

"They are if they could have included flying!" I exclaimed.

The driver looked back at me and gave me a look.

"Eyes on the road please," I said, sheepishly.

"Whatever you say you weirdo American," he said, directing his eyes back on the road. Even though we were in America.

I groaned and stared out the window. Aegis had an idea on how to get to downtown. Unfortunately, that idea was trash.

It meant taking a forty-five-minute cab ride. The cab was extremely cramped, which is saying a lot because I was alone. It smelled like cheese and sweat. Plus, the driver was listening to jazz. Why jazz?

And on top of all of that, I couldn't pay. Aegis had said that she had a plan on what I could do when we reached our destination, but she hadn't told me what.

And in the meantime, what was I supposed to do?

You could learn more moves, Aegis said, reading my mind. Or maybe it was so obvious that I was bored that she knew what I was thinking.

"Okay. That would come in handy," I admitted. The earpiece transformed into a tacky pair of sunglasses. I put them on.

A video popped up in my visor. There was a black screen and white letters appeared saying "Sonic Blast". I heard faint music in the background. The words faded away and showed the suit banging its two hands together and performing a sonic wave that knocked back all of the enemies.

The video slid away, like some bad slide transition video made by middle schoolers, and was replaced by another black screen and white letters saying "Stealth Mode". It was replaced by the video and showed the suit go invisible. Wait, no. Correction. The video showed the suit go into some sort of camouflage mode. You could see where the suit started and ended, mostly because of the less vibrant color on the suit.

The video spun away and erupted in confetti. Once the confetti was gone, there was a new video that bounced around the visor.

"Really, Aegis?" I asked, referring to the annoying transitions.

Isn't that what you are used to?

I paused. She was kind of right, in her own weird way. "Well, yes, but it doesn't make it any less annoying."

Well, this is the last of the moves.

"Really? That's it?" I asked.

"What are you talking about?" the driver looked at me. "We're still 20 minutes away from the address you gave me."

I sheepishly pointed at the road, intending for him to stop asking questions and pay attention to the road. He rolled his eyes and went back to driving.

"Aegis, that's it?" I carefully whispered this time.

Yes, in fact, it is.

"What happened to all those videos at the warehouse?"

There are only a couple of skills, but most of those videos were combinations of them.

"Okay, I guess. What's the last move then?"

The video started. The suit knelt down and threw up? There was some weird, green/brown goo-like substance on the ground, and it probably wasn't illegal. The humans (soooo dumb, right?) ran over to the suit and got stuck in the blob.

I had seen enough.

"Turn that off!" I told Aegis.

Is the torturing of humans too much for you?

"No. Well, yes. But that's just gross."

It's called glob.

"It didn't need a name, Aegis."

It kind of does. In case you ever need to use it.

I sighed. This was going to be a long trip.

*

"WE'RE HERE," THE DRIVER SAID. I glanced out the window, desperate to see what I was being rewarded for a forty-five-minute trip in the smelliest cab you have ever smelled.

I expected another abandoned warehouse. Or maybe a huge building in the shape of a pentagon. Or another shape. Any other shape.

Instead, there was an office building. At most, it was a tall office building. But how could this be where the aliens were trapping Chelsea?

"Uh... sir? I think we might be at the wrong place," I said, eyeing the nicely trimmed grass and the large number of cars in the parking lot.

"We aren't. This is the address you gave me."

"But-"

This is it Alex. The tracker is being disrupted for some reason, but this is where it last read their location.

I sighed. "Never mind. Thanks for the trip."

"Whatever. That'll be a hundred and twenty-nine dollars and ten cents," the driver said impatiently.

Right. I had forgotten about that.

"About that..." I started.

"What?"

"Um," I stalled. Suddenly, a card appeared in my hand. "Here," I said, giving it to him.

He took and examined the card. "Aren't you a little too young to have a credit card?" he asked.

"Aren't I a little too young to get driven to a new place by a stranger?" I challenged.

"Fine."

I grinned. He swiped the card and gave it back to me. "You're on your own, kid."

I shrugged. I definitely wasn't.

He got back into the car and drove away. There was a clink of metal and the suit formed around me.

"Not now!"

How come?

"What if this is just a normal office with normal people?"

Fine. The suit contracted back into the earpiece.

I walked to the door and pulled on it. I pulled harder. It didn't budge. "Aegis. I think the door is locked." I stepped back and scanned the door. It looked normal.

I tried to push the door this time. It didn't give way. "I think we need another way in."

Like what?

I looked up. The roof was awfully high. I might have been able to super jump onto it. And there were a lot of windows. I could break one of them. But that might alert the aliens.

"Okay. The roof it is. Power up!" I said, extending my arms.

What?

"You were supposed to put the suit back on. Power up!" I exclaimed, doing it again.

We're not doing that.

"Fine. Just put on the suit." The suit wrapped itself around me and my body surged with power. "Okay. Super Jump!"

I propelled myself upwards, hoping to get enough altitude to reach the roof, which was coming extremely close. My head popped over it and I expected the rest of my body to. Except, I started to fall. I quickly lashed out a hand and grabbed a hold of the ledge, with the rest of my body dangling.

"Aegis!" I yelled, staring at the ground.

There's a window below you.

"Okay." I carefully put my feet onto the little ledge. I used all of my strength and kicked it open, shattering the glass, probably because of the suit. I put my legs through the broken window, so I was sitting. I wiggled my arms through the window and came up standing, extremely impressed with my parkour skills.

And then I saw what else was in the room.

*

THE ALIENS WERE ALL FACING ME, THEIR WEIRD excuse for eyes widening. So much for stealth.

"Hey there guys. What's up?" I asked, trying to stall.

One of the aliens moaned and… well, not really moaned. He yelled, kind of, but it sounded like a moan. It was probably meant to be a war cry to rally his fellow aliens, but I mean, it was a moan.

Apparently, the other aliens didn't seem to think it was. In fact, they thought it was a battle cry because three of them rushed at me at once.

"Woah!" I yelled. "Aegis! A move, please!"

The fastest alien reached me and swung an energy sword that had materialized out of thin air at me. I ducked and backed away.

He swung upwards this time and I had to dive to the side. I stood up and jumped away from a spear that would have made me into a kebab.

"Sword!" I yelled. The somewhat familiar sword, Athena, appeared in my hand. I held it in both hands and got into a battle stance. The spear got stabbed at me again. This time, I dodged the point and swung my sword at the shaft, hoping to snap it into two.

Instead, the sword clanged against it and I got thrown back.

"Ow," I muttered. "What was that?"

The shaft's made of a similar metal as your suit.

"Of course it is."

Another alien, one with an ax, swung at me. I raised my sword to try to deflect it. It didn't work. His ax was much more powerful than my sword and his swing was way stronger than mine. My sword got thrown out of my hands and hit the ground about ten feet away.

The alien got ready for another swing. I quickly shouted at Aegis for a shield and raised it towards the alien.

Clang! I got thrown back, thankfully not dead, but not much better.

I got up and spotted a large number of aliens holding back, and even more coming through the door. "Aegis, what are they doing?" I asked.

Trying to wear me down.

"Wait, what?"

After you beat the first round, Aegis said as I sidestepped the spear wielder, *they will send more and more in order to avoid massive damage from my abilities.*

"Great," I said, diving towards my sword and picking it up. I raised my sword and swung it at the spear goon. He rolled to the side and stabbed at me. I dodged it. Behind me, his electric point hit a water dispenser. The water came pouring out and the energy on his spear died out. I started to swing my sword at his stomach but feigned and swung at his legs. He disappeared with a whiff of black smoke.

"Okay, one down," I said, blocking a strike from the sword alien with my shield. "Two to go."

I rolled away from the sword alien and faced the two remaining aliens.

I had one hand in my shield, and the other holding the sword. I held them in a defensive stance, ready for whatever the aliens threw at me. "Lightning taunt!" I told Aegis. I dropped the sword and shield on the ground and raised my hands. There was a crackle and a flash of light. The two aliens averted their eyes at the bright light. I took this advantage to grab my sword and shield, sprint towards them, and slice the sword alien in half.

That only left the ax wielder.

I swung my sword in an upwards arc at him. He somehow blocked it with his ax handle and took a swing at me. I raised my shield just in time, barely avoiding the blow. The force of his swing sent me skidding a couple of feet backward.

I sprinted at him again, this time in a curve, going for his sides. I swung my sword, but he somehow caught it in his hand and took it from me. He grabbed the hilt and chucked it at me like a frisbee. I raised my shield for protection, but the sword stuck to the side and, with his throwing force, cast the shield into the ground. I looked up in time to see him racing towards me with his ax held high.

"Super jump!" I propelled myself upwards in the air, dodging the swing. I broke through three floors and made my way down. "I could use something long ranged!" I shouted at Aegis.

A golden bow appeared in my hand and an arrow in my other.

"Okay," I said, nocking the arrow, and hoping I didn't miss. I pulled back on the string and released when I reached the same floor as before. The golden arrow flew incredibly straight for a terrible shot like me, but I didn't see where it went.

Because I was too busy looking at the ground. Which was coming up extremely quickly.

I clutched the bow and opened my arms, remembering how I had beat death earlier, and glided down to the ground, this time not hitting the floor with my face. I looked up and saw that the arrow was wedged into the alien's energy ax, which looked impossible, but I guess not. Which meant that I missed. Which meant that I still had to beat him.

I mean come on! How hard could this guy be? He must have been an alien boss or something.

Another arrow materialized in my hand. I nocked it and fired at the ax wielder. He swung his ax and it ricocheted onto the ground. I nocked another arrow and fired again. He casually sidestepped this one and snarled at me.

"Dash!" I yelled at Aegis. This had to work. Right?

Aegis activated Dash and I rushed forwards at the alien. Except, I didn't hit him. Instead of that much-preferred alternative, he swung his ax at me, and I went flying to the side.

I groaned and got up.

"Okay buddy," I said to the ax wielder. "Let's end this." I nocked another arrow, aimed it at his head, and fired. He raised his hand to most likely catch the arrow. He was confident that he wasn't going to get hit. I was going to prove him wrong.

"Dash!" I shouted, rushing forwards with a blinding light. He was too occupied with catching an arrow. I ended up smacking the alien in the stomach, or whatever it is they have there. He was knocked back and, just like I planned, hit by the arrow.

Okay, well obviously, I didn't plan that. But it sounds better than "-and he was hit by the same arrow, even though I didn't plan that at all."

He erupted in smoke. The first wave of attackers was over. Which meant I still had to beat the rest.

Three more aliens came running into me. This time, instead of handheld weapons, they literally had hands as weapons. Their hands were half blasters or something.

They raised their hands and giant red energy balls came flying towards me. I dodged one, ducked under another, and used my bow to block the third.

"That's all you got?" I asked. I was about to fire another arrow when I heard a hissing sound. I looked down at my bow and dropped it in surprise. The energy balls contained some sort of acid that was disintegrating the bow!

I gingerly inched away from the bow and looked at the aliens once more. "Okay. I can play that game too." I raised my hand... and nothing happened.

"Um... Aegis? Do I have those arm blasters?"
No. Why do you ask?

Of course, I didn't have cool acid blasters. Why would I? I didn't have the cool powers that the aliens had. Like flying. And now acid-energy-arm-blasters!

"Never mind," I said. "Sonic blast!" I exclaimed, trying out the new move that Aegis had shown me on the ride here.

I crashed my two hands together and there was a sonic blast that erupted from my hands and knocked back the attackers. Two of them flew back into the large crowd of aliens, while the other somehow dived to the side of the blast and evaded the attack.

He snarled at me and shot another of those energy things at me. I rolled to the side and raised my fists.

He charged at me, apparently not caring that his weapon was a long-ranged weapon. I ran at him too, my arms pumping.

"Glob!" I yelled at Aegis. A green glue shot out of my hands and was left behind as I ran ahead.

The alien got his arm ready to swing. Just before I was close enough, I stopped running and jumped to the side. He swung his arm, missing and falling onto the glob that I had left there. He struggled to get up, trying to wiggle out of it.

I turned to the rest of the aliens. "Who's next?" I asked, grinning.

They discussed something and another three aliens stepped up. Two of them had tridents and the one in front, their leader maybe, had an energy spear.

"This is going to be easy," I said, confidently. "Especially if your weapons are for cooking marshmallows."

The two aliens growled at me.

I noticed some of the aliens still in the crowd doing some sort of sign language. I had no idea who it was for, so I let them be.

"And you. Your spear is-" I was interrupted by a whooshing sound. I managed to turn around and see the alien still trapped in the glob aiming his arm cannon at me.

And then I blacked out.

*

I SAT UP, GROANING. Where was I? Why did my head feel so dead? I shielded my eyes from the sun. Wait. Sun? What happened to the office building?

My eyes adjusted to the brightness. The office building was right in front of me. Which meant I was on the sidewalk.

I went to rub my eyes. And I did. Successfully. Which meant I didn't have my helmet. One look down confirmed I didn't have my suit.

"Aegis?" I asked.

There was no answer.

My suit was gone. Aegis was gone. I was so screwed. How was I supposed to save Chelsea without the suit?

I slapped myself to get awake. It wasn't as great as the alien painkillers, but it did the job.

Even without the suit, I could still save her. There were other ways to get into a building.

I stood up. I needed to get back inside. The doors were probably still locked. I looked at the place where I had super jumped. There was a loud commotion coming from there. I heard thunder and there was a flash of light. Then, a golden arrow shot out from the window that I had broken. They were using Aegis.

I needed to get her back. Or whatever gender she was.

But there was no way to get back into the building. That I knew of.

I stared into the sky, trying to think. I heard a yell. I shifted my gaze and saw an alien bringing in a middle-aged man into the office building. They were capturing humans for some weird reason.

I could use that.

I waited for the next alien to fly by and ran after it. "You're so fat that you have more folds than a piece of origami!" I yelled at it.

The alien stopped flying and looked at me with confusion.

"You're so fat that your yearbook pictures are taken by a helicopter!"

He tilted his head, obviously bewildered.

"Fine," I said. "You're an alien and you don't belong on Earth!"

The alien's eyes went wide, and he flew straight at me. He picked me up and brought me through a concealed window that I didn't see the first time. In the room was an energy cage and a table with some chairs. He pressed a button and dumped me in the energy cage. I landed with a grunt and sat up, disoriented. It was incredibly dark. I could barely make out the other people in it.

"Alex?" I heard a voice. It was definitely Chelsea.

I turned in the direction of her voice and was enveloped in her arms. I wrapped my arms around her. She smelled amazing, like strawberries and springtime, despite being in an energy cage with a bunch of other smelly people.

"Alex! You're here!" she said, burying her face into my shoulder. A wisp of her blond hair fell onto my hand.

I had done it. I had found her.

"Of course," I said. "Why wouldn't I?"

"Because! That means you were captured. Right?"

"Yeah."

"So we're going to die together."

"What? We're not going to die!" I exclaimed, pulling away from her. "I came to save you!"

"By getting captured?" she asked.

"Well, yes."

"Besides, there are no ways out. It's an energy cage."

That's where she was wrong. Also, that part about us dying. We weren't going to die.

I pulled out a small bottle of water from my hoodie pocket.

"What are you doing?"

"Saving us," I said.

"What?"

I opened the bottle and poured it on the front of the energy cage. The blue glow blinked and stopped.

All of the other prisoners looked at me, puzzled. They stood up and ran out of the cage.

"How did that work?" Chelsea asked.

"I had a hunch," I shrugged. It was true. I wasn't sure that it would work the same. I remembered that the energy of the spear had fizzled out when it hit the water, so I assumed it would be the same. It was.

Everyone was out except us. We carefully stepped out of the cage and ran for the door.

One thing down. Now all I had to do was to get a large group of people out of an office building surrounded by aliens.

Easy.

I made my way to the front of the crowd. Chelsea followed me. I opened the door cautiously, expecting an attack.

There wasn't one. I walked out of the room and gestured for the others to follow. We came out into a hallway. Which way were we supposed to go?

I decided to go right. I walked down the hallway.

I heard a scream. Behind us, there was an alien with an arm cannon. He had it pointed straight at me. There was a flash of light from his ear. Which could only mean one thing. He had Aegis.

"Go! I'll distract him!" I told the others. They didn't hesitate. They ran past me towards the exit.

Chelsea stayed behind and clutched my arm. "No! I can't leave you!"

The alien shot his arm cannon and the red energy ball came out. I dove out of the way, tackling into Chelsea. I pushed her into a room and slammed the door, locking it.

"Sorry," I mouthed at her through the small window in the door. But she couldn't get hurt. I turned to face the alien. There were two others coming to his aide.

"Alex!" I heard Chelsea's muffled voice from beside me.

A red energy ball flew straight at my face, spinning in all different ways that were impossible. It was getting bigger. Wait, no. It was getting closer.

"Duck!" Chelsea screamed at me.

I turned to check on the others. They had reached the exit and were tugging on the door. It was locked.

It was up to me. I was the last one defending the oncoming onslaught. It meant that everyone in here, and maybe the Earth, was depending on me. Which maybe put a little too much pressure on me. And if I lost, the entire world would be gone.

The red energy ball was close enough that I could see lightning bolts flashing inside of it.

I quickly sidestepped the energy ball at the last second. There were sighs of relief from behind me.

More aliens appeared. There were five of them now. And they all had their arms up. Which meant they were all going to attack at once. Or you know, attack one at a time like nice people.

Yeah, I didn't think so.

"EEUHH!" one of the aliens yelled. They all fired one after another, all aiming for my face.

I had a split second to think before I would be roasted alive. I think. I didn't know exactly what would happen.

I realized that all of the energy orbs were headed to my head. The people in my gym class had so bad of aim that it was hard to beat them. While these guys were too good at aiming. All I had to do was sidestep where I was standing and I would dodge all of the balls at once.

I ducked under the barrage of energy balls. I had done it.

Except, not quite. The other people standing directly behind me were in danger. I turned around, expecting a large number of dead bodies. The energy balls got close, but thankfully collided with each other and erupted in a flash of red light.

"Go into one of the rooms!" I yelled to the others. They didn't need to be asked twice. They all quickly ran into the nearest room and closed the door.

"EEUHH!" the aliens yelled. They each had an energy ball charged up and were ready for round two. They all fired their energy blasters, and this time they didn't make the same mistake of aiming at the same place. Even with only five of them, in the small hallway, it was hard to find a place with no energy balls incoming.

I studied the incoming fire. There was a small area between the blasts. If I could just move over there…

Chelsea had seen it too. She was desperately pointing at the place and yelling inaudible things.

Only, I couldn't move. My legs were frozen. *Why now?*

"Move!" Chelsea mumbled. She probably didn't mumble, but it sounded like it because of the door in between us.

The energy balls were almost on to me. I tried to move again. No luck.

I looked at Chelsea, who was staring at me in horror. I smiled at her.

"NO!" she yelled.

I closed my eyes and braced for impact. I couldn't do this without Aegis. Without her, I was nothing.

"Alex! Please!" Chelsea shouted, her voice cracking. "Don't die!"

I could hear the crackle of the energy orbs.

"Come on kid! I'm gonna lose money if you die! And a lot of other stuff!" an ugly voice said from behind me.

Mr. Alienable? What was he doing here?

"Please! You have to save us!" another voice said.

"Move it!" a shout erupted. "Move it!"

Everyone was chanting for me. Everyone was believing in me. I couldn't let my team down.

Not this time.

I opened my eyes and moved to the side. The orbs whizzed past me and erupted before hitting the citizens who were chanting for me.

"EEEUUHHHH!" the alien shouted for the third time. The aliens got their blasters ready. I glanced behind me. The crowd was still chanting, except just a little more scared. But more importantly, there was a table. With a potted plant.

I remembered how the energy orbs had exploded when coming into contact with something else. I could use that. I grabbed the potted plant and flung it at the aliens before they could fire.

One of the alien's orbs hit the plant and exploded, causing a chain reaction. The energy balls exploded in the aliens' faces, or whatever they have there, and killed them.

I had done it. No. Correction. We had done it.

I unlocked the door that Chelsea was locked in.

She kicked me. "I hate you," she said, transitioning into a hug. "But that was awesome."

"Yeah," I grinned.

Mr. Alienable came over to me. "Congrats kid. But don't let this go to your head. You're still a horrible dodgeball player."

"Thanks, Mr. Alienable." Maybe he wasn't too bad.

"We still need to get out of here," one of the people said.

"I know just what to do," I said.

I walked over to where the aliens just were and picked up the golden earpiece. It shined as soon as I touched it.

"What is that, Alex?" Chelsea asked me.

I grinned. I put the earpiece in my ear and heard the familiar metal clang.

"Watch this."

*

DARKNESS. A huge figure stared at a pitch-black landscape... Or, at least, it would be pitch black if there wasn't fire and lava everywhere. Not to mention the bright transparent human screams that littered the entire planet. Oh, how he wished for the green hills and bright skies of Earth. The bright yellow sun that filled the planet with life, not darkness. But more importantly, he wished for revenge. Revenge on the humans who had wronged him. Revenge on the gravestones of the members who had thrown them into custody. But most of all, he wanted revenge on Aegis.

The huge figure was met by a scrawny one, especially compared to him.

"Sir," the tiny figure said. "Have you heard the news?"

"Aegis has found her human attachment," a dark voice boomed. "A male called Alex."

"Yes, master! She and the human host took down squad 2-8B," a tiny, scrawny voice said.

"So nothing of value has been lost," the figure turned.

"I wouldn't exactly say that," the scrawny voice barely whispered.

"Then what would you say?" The voice grew menacing. "Squad 2-8B couldn't take down Aegis. So they aren't needed."

The tiny scrawny figure shrunk down, afraid of the menacing one in front of him.

"But, sir, none of the squads have the capability to take down Aegis," he said, pronouncing Aegis with a long 's.'

"So none of the squads are needed. Whereas I am." The booming voice stood.

"You? Sir? Your-"

"My suit is fully functional. It may not have the capabilities of a fully connected Aegis, but I have exterminated my human host. I have an advantage."

The huge figure stepped into the light, revealing a suit of his own. His suit was much bigger than Aegis, and instead of the bright gold and white, he had black and dark red. At his waist, you could see a whisper of a black, ragged cape, and at his shoulders were two swords of darkness.

"I will exterminate Aegis and the human host if it's the last thing I do. Humans will be cast aside and live in this place," he said, glancing back at the rugged wasteland. "And we will take back our Earth!" he boomed, so loud that bat-like creatures awoke from hiding and flew to him. "We will take what is ours!"

There was a split second of silence. And then all of the aliens within ear range, which was quite a lot, screamed and yelled and banged on their shields in agreement.

"That was quite impressive sir, but, how are you going to take down the original? It has powers far more… advanced than yours." The scrawny man shrank even lower. "Sir," he added, trying to avoid punishment.

"I will easily destroy Aegis. It doesn't matter the abilities, the human host is inexperienced. And you," he said, lowering to meet the gaze of the scrawny man. "Call me Storm."

The Brat

By   Jo - Anne   Barton

"COME AND SIT BESIDE ME ON THE COUCH," HER MOTHER HAD *said.*

Surprised at being spoken to, Sarah obediently got up off the floor were she'd been playing with Teddy. She didn't know what her mommy wanted, and she was a little afraid.

"Leave the bear, you don't need it." The command was quiet and flat but very clear.

Sarah's fear grew as she stopped to put Teddy on the coffee table and then climbed onto the couch beside her mother.

"You never do anything for me. You're nothing but a rotten, spoiled brat. Brats need to be taught how to behave. Now I don't want to hear a sound from you, not one peep. Do you understand?" Her mother's grasp tightened as she spoke.

Sarah nodded but kept her head down.

"Now, where shall I pinch you? Should it be here? Or should it be here?" Her

mother's hand hovered over Sarah's cheek, slowly moving down to her knee before settling on the tender flesh of the upper arm.

Sarah knew better than to ask why she was a brat. Desperately she thought about what she should have been doing for her mother. Next time she would remember to ask what mommy would like her to do, before she played.

"Now, should I pinch you here? Or here?" The hand was close to her ear, stopping again on her upper arm before settling on the tender inside of her thigh. Sharp pain made her cry out.

"Shut up! Stop that crying right now. If you cry I'm going to pinch you."

At that moment the back door opened and Sarah heard her Aunt Ann calling out, "Karen, are you home? I brought some coffee cake."

"Get to your room and stay there – brat!" her mother whispered as she shoved Sarah off the couch. Sarah ran to her room, not stopping to pick Teddy up from the table though she wanted to.

*

HER UPPER ARM STILL TINGLED AT THE MEMORY. "Damn it, why do I dwell on all this?" she asked herself as she started the car and headed toward home after a long day at work. "Why can't I just let go of the past? It's like the abuse is burned into my brain."

She'd been twenty-nine when she met Jim, thirty-one when they married. She'd been adamant she didn't want children. She never particularly wanted children and it wasn't until she sought therapy that she realized how strong an influence her mother had been in that decision. Her entire life, she'd listen and nod whenever her mother explained, "The joys of having children are vastly over-rated. The only people who really think raising kids is worthwhile are woman who are too lazy to work." That was the one piece of motherly advice she'd given Sarah – and it was the message she'd hammered home throughout Sarah's life. She'd never been allowed to play "house" at home; she was never given a baby doll to play with.

"I have a great career, and you. I just don't need anything else." This is what Sarah told Jim when the subject came up. She didn't tell him the miserable details of her own childhood, or how she was afraid she'd be an abusive parent. She just insisted her life was full with work, marriage and their lovely house.

Tall and good looking, Jim was a kind man. His family had welcomed her with open arms, and it took a while to really understand that the love and support they all showed each other was real, heartfelt and reciprocated. They often joked that they'd been worried that Jim had some deep dark flaw; it had taken him so long to choose a wife. Once they got to know Sarah, his brothers and sister all said that she and Jim were well matched.

Sarah had always been close to her own brothers and they all knew they could be counted on to help each other out of a jam. Unfortunately, one of her brothers had recently died of a drug overdose and the other was an alcoholic, only ever one paycheque away from homelessness. Sarah helped him out whenever she could, however she could. She blamed their addictions and poor life skills on their childhood.

"You good for nothing brat! You do that again and I'll send you to the home for juvenile delinquent. They'll knock some sense into you."

"Damn it, there I go again – dwelling on this stupid old bullshit! I have to let it go, let it go." Sarah decided to book a few sessions with a therapist she'd seen in the past who had taught her how to replace those old memories with positive, loving thoughts.

After high school, Sarah had turned to booze, drugs and abusive men. For several years she seemed to be heading down the same path as her bothers before joining Alcoholics Anonymous and enrolling in a community college. After graduating, Sarah had landed her first job selling advertising for a small newspaper. Now she was Director of Sales & Marketing for a large group of newspapers. She found the work interesting and exciting. She enjoyed the challenge of meeting sales quotas while coping with ever increasing competition. Despite everything else, Sarah gave her mother full credit for instilling a strong work ethic and insisting Sarah present a positive, sunny disposition to the world.

"No one likes a whiner," was her mother's favorite saying.

"So stop whining and get on with living." Sarah scolded herself as she pulled into a parking spot. She enjoyed the warm sun on her face as she locked the door and headed towards the hospital. It was a perfect fall day. The small town hospital was situated in a park-like setting, with plenty of grass, red and gold leaves rustling in the warm breeze.

She liked going to the hospital. It was bright and clean with original paintings that had been donated by the many amateur artists in the community. The paintings weren't all great, but they added a sense of hominess and warmth to the sterile surroundings.

Smiling and saying hello to familiar faces along the way, Sarah stopped at the desk of the nursing unit.

"Hi, how is she today?" Sarah asked the head nurse.

"Oh, Mrs. Norton, your poor mom had a rather bad night. She woke up several times from nightmares and they had to give her a sedative to help her sleep. She stayed in bed all day today."

"Is she still asleep?" Sarah asked.

"No, she's awake now. You can go in. She's just had her supper. Dr. Kranz should be finishing his rounds soon. If you wait you can speak to him yourself."

The nurse liked Sarah. She stopped in often and stayed for at least an hour. She was always dressed in expensive, fashionable clothes and high heels. The nurse would have guessed her to be about forty, yet her bubbly personality often made her seemed more like a happy teenager.

Quickly, Sarah slipped into the private room she'd arranged. Her mother was a very proud person and would have hated sharing a room where strangers could see her when she was sick. Gently leaving the door open just an inch, Sarah took off her coat and folded it neatly on a chair, placing the flowers she'd brought on the windowsill beside the bed.

"Hi Mom. They tell me you had a bad night, those nightmares again eh? I know what that's like. They're scary, aren't they?" Sarah's voice was soft, full of empathy and compassion.

"I got a promotion today. The general manger has decided that marketing should be part of the sales department, so now I'm head of both. It's more work, but it's also a twenty percent salary increase and a bigger office." Her mother didn't respond so Sarah continued. "I thought you'd be pleased. I know that my success is thanks to you. You always emphasized that work was important and that raising children was a thankless job."

She continued on in her calm, cheerful voice as she came and stood by her mother's bed. Sitting on the guest chair beside the bed, she eased one arm under her mother's neck to support her head. Picking up a hairbrush from the bedside table, she gently brushed her mother's fine white hair until it shone and lay smooth and tangle-free.

Her mother's eyes didn't open, but she stirred and gave a soft sigh. Sarah watched, thinking her mother looked her best when she was lying down. The excess skin on her face fell back and revealed her bone structure so that you could see hints of the attractive young woman she'd been. The piercing blue eyes were faded now, and those jet-black eyebrows were colorless and thin. The graceful arches had fallen long ago. It took a bit of effort to see the strong and powerful mother of her childhood within the thin, frail body.

Gently lifting the blankets and pulling them down to the foot of the bed, Sarah kept her eyes on her mother's face as she pushed up the sleeves of the hospital gown. An IV tube ran into the back on one hand, otherwise she was free of any restraints. Touching her mother's arm, Sarah bent down to bring her lips close to her mother's ear as she heard herself whisper, "Now, where shall I pinch you?"

The New Build

By Caz Little

MONDAY, OCTOBER 3RD.

John has a problem with the lift. I have a problem with John.

A requirement of my position at Apollo Corp is to judge every HR case with equal sincerity and compassion; standards I hold myself to with strict conviction, but when it comes to John... John has a long history of problems. Since the introduction of a Suggestion Box back in '98, it has remained brimming with suggestion slips signed by John. I don't believe he misunderstood the direction of *Anonymous Suggestions*, rather, he ignored it outright. Once the slips ran out, the post-it notes followed, then the torn notebook pages, a napkin, the back of an old receipt. All of John's suggestions pertained to the cleanliness of Apollo Corp and his dissatisfaction with other employees. Endless complaints about the lunchroom sink or the state of the women's toilets. A hand print smeared on a window, a piece of rubbish that hadn't quite made it into the bin. One would think John would rather the building be perfectly clean before he arrived at work.

John was hired as the sole crew member of Maintenance, long before my time at Apollo began. The sole member not by want of the company, but through the determination of John. Every new hire fled, barely into their contracts; nearly all sighting John as the agitator. I can only imagine why they have kept him on for so long. Perhaps Mr. Founder feels a certain duty towards the old man. Needless to say, John will leave on his own terms, when *he* chooses to retire. Which does not appear to be anytime soon.

A soft hum emits from the new computer under my desk. Since the company saw the necessity of an HR department, John's complaints have migrated from the suggestion box to my inbox and he has become quite the attention attracter; that is, he distracts my attention regularly. The fancy twenty-seven inch monitor in front of me only illuminates the complaints more brilliantly than before. Two days have passed since the move to the Orion Business Park and I have been waiting for John to complete his first shift with morbid curiosity. Today, his inevitable email addressed simply to the HR department, reads as follows:

To Who it Concerns,

This is a formal complaint about the new place. A nasty prank were played on me last night during me shift. I were early, like instructed - which were a right hassle by the way - met Mr. F in the lobby and went through some tedious issuing of ID cards and stacks of keys. Dunno why any building needs so many blooming locks. Well Mr. F left the building about 9 o'clock. I went about familiarizing myself with the Ground floor and Maintenance lock up. Bloody building's like a maze. By time I found the damn service lift - which isn't on any floor plan thank you very much - it were getting on 10 o'clock. And as for the lift, it's a crime the state that gate is in. Me old fingers near broke off pulling the rusty thing open. Not right they spend all this money on fancy floors and computers, but they won't upgrade a lift for the likes of me.

So I'm standing in there, making me way up to 6th. Lift starts making this groaning noise. So I'm praying the damn cables don't snap and send me plummeting down to the Basement, whens I hears something in 'ere with me. Can't have been much past 10 still - you know it gets dark this time of month by 5 o'clock. Didn't even see him till I reached 6th. Bloody great eyes staring at me. The size of that smile, gawking he was. Didn't break eye contact, not once. Didn't even blink. Just stared at me. A bloody great face looming out the darkness. Me heart near stopped there and then.

That's when it dinged at the 6th floor. I wrenched that gate open, like I had the strength of ten men behind me, I did. Kept me eyes fixed on that lift all night as I worked me way round the office. I still did me job! Cleaning round all night, knowing, I gotta step back in there once me time were up. And I did it mind you. Can't call me a coward. Wheeled my trolley right back in there and turned me back on him. Didn't wanna give him the satisfaction you see. Just kept me eyes fixed straight ahead on that rusty, old gate. Still heard him there, shuffling about behind me. Left Apollo a shell of a man I did. The fright it gave me and on me very first night and all.

Now, I dunno who organized that little stunt or how they pulled it off, but I'll be back tomorrow for me shift and I best not see the man in the lift again. It's all fun and games to you corporate types, but I'm not playing.

Yours,

John Dobbs

A fairly standard email from John; a little more cryptic than usual, but I do not expect him to be at the top of his game after only one shift. Addressing the service lift, Mr. Founder himself inspected the facilities during negotiation of the new build. His detailed written account states the lift was in perfect working order: compact, but spacious enough for two people and a cleaning cart, and not to mention subject to a beautiful view. At no point did he use the words rusted or groaning. Typical John, catastrophizing everything. To further elaborate: the Orion Business Park is compiled of four high-rise buildings. Each new structure, composed of six floors and mezzanine on Level 2, boasts two glass facades on the East and West sides. Apollo Corp now resides on the 6th floor of building 208. The two glass lifts used by guests and employees located to the West of 208 look out across the state-of-the-art business park. The service lift is over on the East side of the building and has a wonderful vantage point of our fine city and Centennial Bridge.

Of course the upgrade comes with some adjustments; we share the new build with Artemis Ltd, who occupy all of 2nd and 3rd floors. Although I am unaware as to the nature of their business, I would assume they have their own Housekeeping staff, as we were told the building did not supply their own.

Another man in the lift? Hardly a prank. All this upset over sharing a lift with another company's employee. As always, I have responded politely to John, explaining the logistics of co-leasing. I made a point to highlight the architectural prowess of the new build; so much more modern. How can he be distracted by a lift companion, when he can watch the sunrise over the city at the end of a shift? I dare say some people would find it enviable. I will follow up in a couple of days when the dust has settled, until then, I am closing the complaint.

*

TUESDAY, OCTOBER 4TH.

I arrived this morning to another email from John. The subject bar reads: The Man in the Lift.

To Who it Concerns,

He's still 'ere. Last night I got back in that rusty old box, mentally prepared. No hint of fear. I gave nothing away. Stood in silence staring through the gate. Counting the floors going past. I steps out at 6th, all ready for a hard nights work. That's when he started. Right as me foot hit the carpet. Started off small enough, but he got louder and louder. A laugh what would shake the heavens. My God, me ears were ringing from it. He got louder and me heart got heavier. Don't ask me how I know, but there were evil in that laugh.

Tried to busy myself all night, I really did, but it were so loud. Me entire shift he howled through the gate. Never stopped for breath. How some neighbouring building didn't hear, I don't know. I kept expecting the Old Bill to show up. Me poor hands were shaking so much by the end, I couldn't hold me mop steady. Couldn't empty the bins without chucking rubbish everywhere. You can't blame me for the mess I left, I did me best under the circumstance. Do something about the man! I ain't slept since I got home. Me tinnitus is playing havoc with me head 'cause of him. This is some cruel harassment you lot got going on!

John

I have re-opened the complaint. True, John does have a history of clashes with other employees. This is not the first time a younger member of staff has encountered John, and realizing he is easy to rile, had their fun pushing his buttons. Historically John would have given them a piece of his mind, often with language too colourful to record. The man cannot be beat in an argument. I have witnessed him filibuster his way out of the most explicit situations, so why not this time? Perhaps, he felt his frailty last night, alone with a stranger in an unfamiliar place. John was part of the furniture at the old building; he knew every nook and cranny. Each floor, perfectly mapped out in his mind; and he did not have to share the space with anyone else late at night. I find myself pitying John: he has never taken umbrage with another person like this before. This move must have had quite a knock on effect.

I have responded as reassuringly as I know how; I do not wish to feed into his melodrama. Unfortunately the power to the main lifts is linked to the servers and shuts down after regular hours, so our options are limited. I have suggested instead that John send his wares up in the service lift and he himself, take the stairs. I must admit, if what John says is accurate, this seems strange behaviour indeed from the man in the lift. Not to mention, openly mocking someone while at work is unacceptable behaviour; and why did the man not leave and attend to his own duties?

I have forwarded a complaint to Artemis Ltd, requesting their employee be more considerate during the night shift. I wonder if across the hall the man from the lift is filing an HR complaint about John.

*

WEDNESDAY OCTOBER 5TH.

Two emails came in from John last night.

To who it concerns,

First you tell me to enjoy the view and now you say take the stairs? You are not understanding me, the bastard's tall! I can't take the stairs, you know fine well me hip won't do it. And enjoy the view? He blocks the bloody view! I'm telling you, he's tall!

Can't believe I never saw it 'til tonight. Turned off all them fluorescents at the end of me shift and gets in the lift, ignoring that horrible face. And I'm looking back at the office, at the morning light creeping in. And that's when I had a funny thought. Soon as I gets to 4th I hit that emergency stop. Bloody machine sent up one hell of a scream! Made such a jolt, me knees went and I ends up in a pile on the floor. Lying there, in the dark. I mean, total darkness. It were pitch black. Not a snip of light come through that glass. All these days and I never wondered why it were always so dark on 4th.

That groaning noise were even louder 'ere. Pulling out me torch, I'm thinking maybe some builder or window cleaner's put up some tarp or board outside. It were hard to work out at first when I shone me light on it. Like some kind of fabric were stretched across the glass. Leathery like. Thick. Little bumps all over it and thick, black threads poking out.

Stared at that canvas for ages I did. Trying to make heads or tails of it all. 'Til it grumbled. I mean the whole damned thing rippled across the glass. A great rumbling coming from other side. God help me. I have found the belly of the beast.

I have recommended John takes time off. Clearly this move has had a bigger impact on the old man than we could have imagined. Though Mr. Founder seemed unmoved when I pled John's case this morning, and was most displeased at my suggestion of paid leave, I am of the strong belief that this is what John needs and I fought hard in his corner. And a fight it was; John's reputation does him absolutely no favours. He is a famous pain in the side of many people at Apollo Corp. I thought I was wining Mr. Founder over when I proffered the time off might be the final nudge to ease John into retirement, but it wasn't until the second email arrived while Mr. Founder was still in my office, that he agreed to two weeks leave, under strict instruction that John seek medical attention.

I've seen all of him. I knew those monstrous feet must be beneath, hiding in the basement. Me hips were agony, going down them stairs. Clinging to the banister for dear life by the bottom. There's a thumping down there. On the other side of that door. Like 2 big mattresses being hoisted up and dropped on to concrete. Forgive me old mind; I couldn't open the door. The fear froze me where I stood. Just the thought of him having feet were too much to bare. Couple times the thumping stopped, and there were this other sound, like giant sandbags being pulled across the floor.

The rest weren't so bad, I already spent nights getting in on Ground where his hairy legs stood thick as old oaks. Up to his rumbling belly and chest on 4th. Heaving, breathing, hiding great, unearthly lungs. All the way to that face on 6th. But I ask you, where are the bloody thing's arms? Can't find 'em. Dear God help me. I can't think about those hands and where they hide.

*

FRIDAY OCTOBER 14TH.

Jon has been on leave for two days and we are currently interviewing for a replacement. Mr. Founder took no time in beginning the search for a new Maintenance crew; it almost felt cold the speed at which the job posting went out.

I keep catching myself thinking about John, whenever I find a lull in the day's activities, which is often, now I don't have John filling up my inbox. As it transpires, the move has been a huge success. We are already seeing work flow improvements across the board and office morale is soaring. Everyone has taken to the new build like a duck to water. I, on the other hand, am starting to feel a little redundant.

*

MONDAY OCTOBER 17TH.

Today I arrived to a voicemail on my extension. It came through on Sunday October 16th, at 3:21AM.

> *"Dear God he had me! Reached out and took me up! I didn't see it coming! Had to go back, I shouldn't have done it, but I had to. I gotta prove to my Janelle I ain't crazy, me daughter thinks I've cracked. But Hell's gate is in 'ere. He has fallen and come through to destroy Apollo! Christ, get out! Get out of the building! The Devil is in 'ere and he can move..."*

This is when the noise drowns out John's voice. I still can't decipher it, cannot relate it to anything I have heard in my thirty-two years on this earth. A horn perhaps, or some similar instrument, capable of unearthly volume. All I do know, after listening to John's voicemail for the twenty-first time, I am still gripped by complete fear when it sounds. A fumbling and a clatter follow the noise. I do not know where John was when he dropped the phone, but I have searched the pathways and car parks all around the Orion Business Park and I cannot find it. When I dial recall, the phone is now off or dead. All I can do is replay the message and hope some clue to John's whereabouts might suddenly reveal itself. I hear his voice over and over, fading into the distance: "he's got me…"

*

TUESDAY OCTOBER 18TH.

My inbox has laid empty for days. I turned off the spam filter yesterday just to feel relevant again, but not even the scammers want to harass me. At 2PM that familiar *swoosh* notified me of new mail. My heart raced in the vein hope it would be the crazy ramblings of John weaving some new ludicrous tale, but it was from Artemis Ltd. They currently do not have a night shift employee and are unaware that 208 has a service lift.

*

WEDNESDAY OCTOBER 19TH.

John has been missing for two days. Yesterday, we had a call from his wife, a Mrs. Janelle Dobbs, asking if we had seen or heard from him. I did not mention the phone call… I really don't know why. I don't think they would believe me; I am struggling to believe myself these days. Instead, I have concluded to investigate for myself.

I have been sitting at my desk, watching people slowly filter out of the office as the sun sets and the night takes hold. I check every desk, office and board room on 6th; all are empty. The lights appear to be out on 3rd and

2nd as I make my way down to the basement. Pressing my ear to the heavy wooden door, I hear nothing. Not a sound. Just the low hum of fluorescent bulbs above me. I try the handle and to my secret relief it is locked; an involuntary sigh of relief escapes me. I cannot confirm the emptiness of the room, but I am so very relieved that I don't have to.

John is right about the service lift; I was thorough when checking the building floor plans and blueprints provided by the Orion Business Park, it is not recorded on any of them. I tread through the maze of corridors down on Ground that I did not know existed, for what feels like hours. I am sure this is the East side of the building, but it is so hard to tell, lost in a labyrinth of magnolia walls; however did John find his way? There is a peculiar smell to these hallways; damp and mouldy... I thought this building was new. Finally I see it, a dilapidated old service lift, at the end of a solitary corridor. This is undeniably the one; its rusted scissor gate, streaked with silver where John had been pulling it open and closed all these nights. I look with childish fear into the small dark space beyond, my cheeks flushed with embarrassment, but of course, I see nothing. An empty square, barely big enough for one man and a trolley. Sheepishly I tug at the gate; it responds with a dull screech, but does not give. My embarrassment deepens at the realization that I have been completely taken in by an old, sick man's delusions. Suddenly the panic over the basement door feels utterly stupid. What a fool I have been. I slump to the floor, defeated, and gaze off down the grubby corridor. My thoughts are lost on poor John. What was the right course of action? Where could he be now? I hope he is safe. His poor wife.

In my dream a giant spider crawls towards me.

Movement snaps me awake; I find myself lying awkwardly on the floor. This whole saga must have driven me to exhaustion. Imagine if Mr.

Founder had discovered me here, sleeping in a hallway; how would I explain this? I have no idea how long I have been here next to the service lift, but I am suddenly aware of the cramp in my leg. Steadying myself on the wall I attempt to stretch it out, but my foot is stopped by a pillar. More accurately, my foot makes contact with one of the *four*, towering pillars now assembled around me. Staggering to my feet, I press back into the wall, which now gives and envelopes my back like memory foam. My senses are overloaded, staring in confusion at the knobbly pillars; a sudden realization hits. Fear flows down me like ice water, and I begin to understand the reality of my situation. Tears start to fall; I sob quietly, and look up at the great, arching palm above me, confirming the nature of this cage of flesh I have woken up in. The hand starts to close around me.

My only thought is of John.

A Scar too Deep to Heal

By   Chris   Cobb

IT HAD BEEN A BAD NIGHT ALREADY. Then the baby started to wail in the next room.

Three a.m.

Colic.

She turned her head on the pillow.

He was back in Afghanistan again. Whatever he was hearing, it wasn't the baby.

The muscles in his face were going through their usual contortions. His legs and arms flayed. He looked like he was living through a horror movie.

His pillow felt like she'd forgotten to put it in the dryer. She could feel the dampness seeping over to her side of the bed, from head to toe.

Another night, another change of sheets.

Most nights he doesn't come to bed at all. Just flops down drunk on the old couch in the basement or sleeps in his chair with his head hanging over the keyboard of his computer.

She went to see to the baby. The older kids in the bunk beds on the other side of the room hadn't stirred. They could sleep through anything. Or on the worst nights could at least pretend. She envied them.

She took the baby downstairs to the couch. She had his military-issue sleeping bag waiting, as usual. It was warm, comfortable, and comforting. The baby seems to sense it. She snivelled a little, then took a few jerky breaths like babies do when they're coming down from upset and fell asleep inside the cocoon with her mother.

From upstairs, familiar sounds filled the silent night.

Sounds of rage and screams of fear.

Like last night. Like tomorrow night.

She drifted to sleep, wondering if it was ever going to end.

Wondering how long she was going to be able to take it.

Wondering whether the fun-loving guy she'd married would ever come back.

*

I DON'T KNOW WHAT'S HAPPENED TO ME. And that's the truth.

There's a movie inside my head that's on a loop. It starts as soon as my head hits the pillow and plays over and over. I can't switch it off.

It's like my brain was a video camera every time I was over there. And my eyes were the lens and my ears the microphone.

Hell, I did things yesterday that I can't remember today but the scenes that camera recorded are crystal clear. Not just the pictures but the sound. You want to see horror? Look inside my head.

I know that all seems weird, but I don't know if I can describe it any better. I'm pretty good with words but that slice of weird is out of my grasp.

Even more weird is that Afghanistan was the first time I'd been anywhere. Most people have been to Florida or Mexico or somewhere before they get to be 18. Me? My first vacation was in fear of my life in a God-forsaken desert on the other side of the world courtesy of the army.

How pathetic is that?

I suppose you could say I was in the wrong place at the wrong time.

You see, I had this plan.

There were never any jobs around here – at least none worth having. I'm not stupid. I did OK in school and loved to read. I'd read anything and everything. I love Kurt Vonnegut and read his Slaughterhouse Five about ten times. That's a mean book about another war.

I even read Margaret Atwood although to be honest, I kept that quiet because ... well, you know what teenagers are like. Mention in class that you were reading Margaret Atwood – or Margaret anybody – and it would inevitably lead you to being mocked which would inevitably lead to a fight. I can handle myself – always could – but I don't like fighting. Never did.

Which entitles anybody to question why the hell I joined the armed forces and became a trained killer. Because that's what soldiers are for- at least that's what us grunts are for. To kill and be killed – or worse, get your legs or arms blown off and spend the rest of your life a wheelchair. That's the deal you make. Everyone who joins understands that, even though it dawns on some quicker than it dawns on others. It's the real job description but you won't hear that at the recruitment office. They're all about exotic travel, skills learning and great pay and benefits. Make in sound like they're paying you to go on vacation for ten years.

I've still got my legs and arms so I suppose I can consider myself lucky. I know guys who can't consider themselves so lucky.

I know guys with fewer parts left on their bodies than they were born with.

And I know guys who got welcomed home by wives and kids with hugs, kisses, and tears. Now they're those same guys are the streets scavenging for change from people who ignore them. Probably most of the people doing the ignoring have got 'Support Our Troops' stickers on their cars.

Slogans. I hate fucking slogans. They're propaganda to make us feel good about ourselves – proud of something we don't deserve to feel proud about. It's not like we defeated Hitler and saved the world from tyranny. It's not like we defeated anyone. We just pushed a boulder up the hill until it rolled back over us – and then did it again and again.

Just read a few books. Or just Google it. The Brits tried three times. The Russians tried three times. Back in the day, even Genghis Khan tried. If you believe what you read, the Persians sort of succeeded but got booted out a few years later. That was before Jesus was born, and before IED's so I'm not sure it really counts.

The Russians invaded for the third time in 2019 and were still there ten years later. It cost them 15,000 dead soldiers and 35,000 wounded before the Soviet president Mikhail Gorbachev said 'fuck this, we're getting the hell out' or whatever that is in Russian. Oh yes, and they killed about two million Afghan civilians in those ten years. We always forget that people on other side get killed and maimed.

I'm no political or military genius but if they couldn't do it, why in hell did we think we could? Eleven years we were there either killing them or trying to persuade them to like us. Hearts and minds. Give me a break.

Anyway, I'm ranting to myself again. I've given up ranting to my buddies on the Internet. It was what it was. We knew we weren't going over there to baby sit.

So let me put it this way: I signed up for that exotic travel, skills learning and great pay and benefits they advertised at the recruiting office. I never liked fighting and had no interest in it. I thought we'd play at being soldiers, like Canadian soldiers had done since the Korean War in the 1950s. Decades and decades of practice before it was 'thanks for spending this time with us, enjoy your next job and here's your fat pension.'

Fair enough. Shit happens. It wasn't what I signed up for but it was what I signed up for, if that makes sense.

What I didn't sign up for is to have this horror movie playing in my head night after night.

So yeh, I had a plan.

It just didn't include Osama bin Laden and his cronies flying jets into the World Trade Center.

And it sure as hell didn't include me getting shot at in the desert or seeing the guys I was drinking with last night being blown to smithereens by bombs buried by the side of the road.

And it didn't include me being booted out of the army after nine years because I was considered damaged goods.

We were always at the pointy end of the action in and around Kandahar. The first time, my unit was supposed to be there for three months. We were there for almost five. I couldn't wait to go home, and then I couldn't wait to go back. After the third mission, I didn't even want to come home.

The truth is, I found the risk of driving over an IED less stressful than standing in a line-up at Walmart. Go figure.

Like I say, I don't know what happened to me.

*

NOW HER BRAIN WAS RACING and making sleep only a remote possibility. Move too much and the baby would set off again. Move too little and she felt her muscles might atrophy. So she stayed still, stared at the ceiling.

Dan was barely 20 when they got married. She was 19. They weren't exactly childhood sweethearts but close. They already had Jake when he went to Afghanistan for the first time. It's probably no coincidence that Jenny was born about nine months after he got back from that first tour.

The thing that about Dan that attracted her was his smarts. He'd probably read more books by the time he left high school than most of his teachers put together. And he was funny. Not slap-you-on-the-back, loud funny but he'd observe things and observe people and took great delight in pointing stuff out. They'd go together to the health food store in town and as they were leaving he'd say: 'Have you ever noticed how pale and sickly people who work in health food stores look?" And then he'd do an imitation – what he liked to call a pale imitation.

It was lame but he always had this way about him that could make dumb stuff sound funny. He always made her laugh.

And he loved music – probably loved music as much as he loved his family, truth. The house, the car … everywhere they went he had to have music. It was almost like he felt incomplete without it.

He was never a big drinker. A couple of beers on a Friday and Saturday night was more or less it. Even in their partying days, she'd never seen him drunk. After that first tour, she noticed he was drinking a bit more and had found a taste for rum, which he'd never shown any interest. But she didn't say anything. He still seemed pretty much the same, except for the hours he had started spending on the computer chatting to his army buddies.

Sarah remembered her mom once telling her that getting married is like started a long journey with a stranger who over time you get to know and if you're lucky get to like. Travelling with someone you like, she said, makes any journey easier, and more enjoyable, even though there are times on the journey when you begin to notice changes in that other person. We all change. Some for the better, some for the worse. And sometimes on that journey, you'll come to crossroads. You'll have a choice. Continue together or continue alone.

Sarah was never sure whether her mom read that somewhere or thought of it herself.

But it didn't work quite like that for Sarah. She started the journey with a man she thought she knew and watched him gradually turn into a stranger.

*

THE BOOZE HELPS. DARK RUM. I never tasted it until I was over there, but my buddies drank it. I joined in and sort of got hooked. When I was over there, a belly-full of rum used to help me sleep. Now, I'm not sure whether I sleep at all. I mean, if you sleep, you're not supposed to wake up feeling exhausted are you? That and the stinking hangover that doesn't go away until you feed it with more rum. On recycling day our bin looks like we've been partying with a ship load of sailors.

I know Sarah doesn't like me drinking and that's why I prefer to spend most of my time in the basement. I watch TV, play a few video games, play a few tunes but mostly talk to my buddies in town and across the country. We relate.

Sarah tells me I've turned into Jekyll and Hyde and I know she's right. Except these days I seem to be more Hyde than Jekyll.

I get angry a lot and say things to the kids I shouldn't say. That's what hurts the most.

Last week I told Jake to clean up his room. He's messy and it drives me crazy. He didn't listen to me. Just carried on watching this dumb cartoon. So I lost it. I went into his room, scooped up all his toys and clothes off the floor and threw the lot out of the bedroom window onto the front lawn. Then I went back and screamed at him to get outside and clean them up.

Then Sarah started screaming and crying. He's six, she kept screaming. He's six. He isn't in the fucking army!

After those kinds of episodes, I feel kind of numb and useless and start wishing I'd never come back from Afghanistan. At least, not breathing

I feel like the guy in that song

Sam Stone came home
To his wife and family
After serving in the conflict overseas
And the time that he served
Had shattered all his nerves

Except Sam Stone got hooked on morphine to ease his pain.

Like a lot of guys, I've got PTSD which is a career killer for any young soldier – or anyone with less than 10 years in and shit for a pension. Go ask for help and you're immediately damaged goods because they figure you're not sane enough to shoot straight. Not sane enough. That's a laugh. Trust me. Being nuts helps when you're driving around in a big tin can that you know can get blown to pieces along with you and everyone else. Being nuts helps when you're about to shoot a complete stranger who might, or might not, intend to do the same to you.

Some NCOs and officers don't believe that PTSD exists at all and have this 'suck it up buttercup' attitude. Break an arm or a leg and they'd be all over you with sympathy. Break something in your brain and they're too dumb to realize it's worse. At least broken legs and arms can mend.

It's better for older guys with lots of years in because if they get PTSD, they get a nice chunk of change to go away. Mind you, those same NCOs and officers who are convinced PTSD is baloney are also convinced that guys pretend to have it so they can get out, find a new job and live large for the rest of their lives. It's just a big scam to them. Is there a war in human history that hasn't left a bunch of old soldiers roaming around mumbling to themselves, getting into fights or begging on the streets?

The shrinks say that to get PTSD you need to be exposed to at least one traumatic event. I know what happened to me because like I said, I watch repeats every night. I never talk about it because it's kind of painful and who the hell would care anyway?

I'm going to tell you what happened to me but first I have a bit of history to share.

During the Vietnam War, news reporters were pretty much left to roam where they wanted and report what they wanted. So when people in the U.S. sat down to watch TV news, or read their daily paper, they got a pretty accurate report of what was going on.

There was this news anchor guy named Walter Cronkite. They called him 'the most trusted man in America.' Images from Vietnam were often raw footage of the wounded crying and bleeding being carried on stretchers to helicopters. Someone called it the 'Living Room War' because the millions of Americans who watched TV news back then.

Cronkite sent himself on assignment to Vietnam to see for himself and basically told the American public that the war was unwinnable, and the military and political leaders were screw ups. It wasn't just Cronkite but other reporters too who saw what was going on – the senseless killing and wounding – and basically agreed that it was all a waste of time.

The military and political leaders blamed the news media for undermining the war effort and for losing America the war. Bullshit of course but that's what they said. Fast forward to the first Gulf War in 1990 and a guy called Dick Cheney who was the Secretary of Defence and one of those who blamed the media for stuff that was other people's fault. So during the Gulf War he introduced this concept of embedding reporters which is a fancy way of saying controlling reporters and making sure they only see what the military brass wants them to see. It's basically censorship by another name and was so successful in the Gulf that Americans – or anyone else for that matter – didn't get to see the same nasty images they had seen during Vietnam. Just some sanitized version of reality.

Military brass don't like the public to see their screwups and politicians don't like the public to know how dumb-ass their decisions are so it was no surprise that embedding become an overnight success. Reporters came over to do reporting, were welcomed by smiley public affairs types and left a few weeks later having seen nothing approximating reality. They didn't get taken to the forward operating bases where most of the brutal stuff happened. Mind you, they did get to ride around in armoured vehicles and dodge roadside bombs. They weren't totally insulated.

Roadside bombs. Who came up with that description? Pisses me off. You get this picture of a bomb sitting by the side of the road with wires sticking out of it in plain sight. Not so. They were buried and some freak with a mobile phone and a pair of binoculars was the trigger man.

Here's why I'm giving you this history lesson. The public back home never get to see the real war, just the unreality show that the military brass and politicians want them to see. The more troop supporting stickers on rear bumpers the better. The more references to 'our heroes' the better. Heroes? Bullshit. None of the guys I know fitted that description and none of them wanted it. Like me, all they wanted was to leave that hell hole with their bodies and minds in one piece and a pension.

So, believe it or not, this is what's in that movie that comes on loop when my head hits the pillow.

It was pre-dawn, barely light. We were on a joint mission with some Americans, rolling along dusty dirt roads. There were five armoured vehicles. Two Canadian in front, two at the rear and in the middle a soldier carrier packed with U.S. Special Forces. Tough guys – mostly smallish with faces that looked like they'd never experienced a smile. Being small is an advantage for these elite guys because of the scrapes they have to get in. Being big is no advantage when you have to climb through tiny windows or crawl along floors to surprise people you're going to kill.

Our mission was to surprise and take out a bunch of Taliban. The intelligence guys figured they were responsible for a bunch of roadside bombs planted just outside Kandahar. Someone must have told them we were coming because the middle vehicle suddenly flew into the air in a tunnel of flame, smoke and dust and slapped down again in a million pieces. The explosion took part of the vehicles in front and behind but none of our guys and girls were killed or injured that time. I was in the rear-guard vehicle. When the bomb went off, it was like we were in a mega-earthquake with the terrifying noise of the explosion that felt like it was going to split your ears into pieces.

The poor Yanks wouldn't have known what hit them. There's no point in describing what that scene looked like. If I'm being totally honest, I can't make my fingers write the words. We guarded what was left until the American clean-up crew arrived. I can't imagine how any of those clean up guys survived that scene with their minds in one piece. Or perhaps they were used to it, I don't know.

They launched the so-called Operation Medusa in Kandahar less than a week later to go after the guys who did it. There were 1,000 Canadian Armed Forces members on that operation. The biggest Canadian military operation in 50 years. It was successful to the extent any military operation in Afghanistan was successful. We killed a bunch of them and they killed 12 of ours. Did it change anything?

I know there's no excuse for the way I behave. It is me, but it isn't me.

More than anything else, I want Sarah and the kids to know that I loved them but somewhere along the way, lost the ability to show it – lost the ability to be me. It's like the love and the desire to love and laugh has been sucked out of me.

I'm so tired now. I can't think about it anymore.

*

SARAH HAD BEEN ON THE EARLY SHIFT and arrived home earlier than usual. The kids were at her parents.

She shouted his name. No response.

She assumed he was in the basement with his headphones on, as usual.

She went down the stairs. He wasn't there but his 9 mm Browning was. Next to the pistol was a drained bottle of dark run. They were both on the ground, on top of an old tarp.

She ran upstairs and grabbed her phone. She knew.

The cops and paramedics were there before he got home. He'd been to the liquor store.

One of the cops held him by the arm, as she exploded into a primal scream, and went to hug him. Tears were streaming down the grey, defeated expression on his face.

"I wasn't drunk enough," he said.

Amelia's New World

By   Patricia   Sevigny

IT WAS MOVING DAY AGAIN, AND OF ALL THE MOVING DAYS THAT
Amelia had experienced in her short life, this one would end up like no
other. She dreaded this day, and as her parents packed boxes and the
movers moved furniture, she sat alone staring into space on her backyard
porch. "My life as I know it is officially over!" cried Amelia to herself. A tad
dramatic? Yes, but just as all 15-year-old girls past, present and future,
being dramatic was a prerequisite!

Her world didn't revolve around her parents anymore. She had her
own friends here, which was not an easy task since she was always the 'new

kid on the block.' She had her own interests, basketball being a big one, an 'almost' boyfriend, and even a part-time babysitting job. She didn't want to lose all that and have to start over in a whole new place! It took a lot of time to get to where she was in her school life, and her social life. She was happy for once and felt good about herself.

Amelia was tall for her age, with long, straight dark hair which was almost always up in a ponytail. Her skin was kind of oily, and she would break out at the most inopportune times. Her body was athletic and strong, but not very shapely yet, and she so wished for some shape! Her face still had a child-like appearance and she hated it when adults still called her 'cute.' The freckles on her nose just had to go, but her hazel green eyes could definitely stay. Brendan always complimented her about her gorgeous green eyes! Her strong, athletic body was good because it, along with her height, really helped her excel at her favourite sport.

The big school basketball tournament was tomorrow, but she was going to miss it! Suddenly, her cat Charlie rubbed up against her. Maybe he sensed her sadness, who knows? She picked Charlie up and stroked his head. "Hey Charlie, you sad too? God, I wish dad had a normal job so we wouldn't have to move anymore. I bet you don't like those airplane rides either huh, all cooped up in the carrier like that?"

Amelia's dad loved being in the Armed Forces and was very proud of his high-ranking position, but it came with a price, which of course, was moving. Oh sure, when Amelia was younger, the moves were always fun and exciting adventures with mom and dad. It didn't matter where she was, as long as she was with them. Her mom always liked the idea of exposing her daughter to new experiences, new cultures, and new people, but this time it was different. It didn't feel like another big adventure. This time, she wished so hard for her life to be different, and for something, ANYTHING, to change the fact that she was leaving tonight!

What she heard next was very strange because the sound was coming from the supposedly empty Johnson's yard next door. It was a soft, high-pitched, spa-like music that drew her out of her sadness and made her forget about it for a moment. She put Charlie down and walked quietly over to the hedge, and as she got closer, she spotted an opening that she knew wasn't there before. So, being the curious girl that she was, she walked closer. The music became louder, and she looked through the opening but didn't see anyone. The music seemed to compel her to keep walking and when she got to the small opening, she bent down and crawled right through to the other yard. What she saw next was beyond anything she ever thought possible!

Amelia was shocked when she saw her bike leaning against the house, along with her basketball net, her dad's radio playing the music that she heard from the other side, and most shocking of all, her dad standing at their BBQ cooking burgers for dinner! She was in her own backyard! She looked back through the hedge to the yard that she came from and saw all of the busy activity of the move taking place. *How can this be?* she asked herself as her heart pounded faster and faster.

Just then, she heard her mom calling out to her from over the hedge. "Amelia? Where are you? We have a plane to catch and we have to get to the airport!"

Then, she heard her other mom call out. "Amelia! Come help me make the salad for dinner please."

"What in the?" Her mom was there, looking the same as always, but yet so much more relaxed! Both her parents were smiling and singing to the music seemingly unaware of what just happened to Amelia.

A sense of warmth and peacefulness washed over her as she watched them for a moment, and she couldn't help but smile as she remembered those lazy summer days with her parents.

Amelia may not know what was happening to her, but she did know that if she had a choice, she would choose to stay and make that salad, go for a bike ride with her best friend Annie after dinner and go play in the basketball tournament tomorrow!

Suddenly her peaceful trance was broken. *What should I do?* She thought frantically. She had no time to waste because her real parents were about to leave for the airport!

She took a deep breath and closed her eyes. She heard her moving mother calling for her in a fit of panic. Time stood still. Then she began to back away from the moving mother's voice and the life that she wanted so much to change. "Goodbye," Amelia whispered, "I love you, but I can't do this anymore."

Tears ran down her face and her heart pounded as she watched the hedge opening disappear.

"Amelia, are you ok?" asked her new, yet same parents.

"Y-yes, I guess so. I'll come help you with that salad."

In the kitchen, everything was how she remembered it before all their things got packed up. Her mom was happy and calm, not stressed and running around. It was her face, her clothes, her hair, her voice, her laugh, her smile. It was just her. Amelia helped make the salad and put it out on the table on the back porch. Her dad came with the burgers and sat down with them. It was her dad too, but again, more calm, and stress free. He wore the same weekend clothes he always wore, his hair and face were the same, his smile was the same and it was so nice to see them both smiling again! Amelia took in every detail and began to relax a bit too.

She got her wish. She was staying and she tried to focus on that for the time being. *Who gets to make a wish, and have it come true like this? Is it a dream?* she wondered to herself.

After dinner, she cleared the dishes and headed up to her room to change her clothes. Up in her bedroom, there was a pile of dirty clothes on the floor, posters of her favourite bands on the walls, schoolbooks left open on her desk, and an unmade bed to flop onto. Looking around, she was amazed, yet at the same time, taken over by an eerie sense of uneasiness. She just couldn't put her finger on what it was.

She flopped onto her bed and began to wonder if the other people she cared about would be here, and if they were, would they be the same too? She texted Annie, *"Hey, wanna go for a bike ride?"* She waited for a reply, she waited longer. "Come on Annie, you've gotta be here in this new world!"

Finally, she heard the dingle on her phone, *"Hey, what's up?"* It was Annie, thank God!

"Let's go for a bike ride okay? Can you meet me at my place?"

She waited again for the dingle, *"Sure, I'll be there soon."*

Okay, this is going well, Amelia thought. She was so curious to see what Annie looked like, but her parents were the same, so why shouldn't Annie be? The big question was whether or not she should tell Annie about what happened to her that afternoon. "She'll think I'm crazy for sure!" she said under her breath as she put her helmet on.

"Where are you going?" asked Amelia's mom.

"Just out for a bike ride with Annie! I'll be back before it gets dark!" Amelia called out.

She saw Annie at the end of the driveway waving. She looked weird, which was actually normal for Annie. She was quite short and kind of chubby with long green hair on one side of her head and shaved hair on the other side. She wore oversized clothes and had a piercing on the side of her nose. Amelia's parents would never let her pierce her nose or anything other than her ears until she turned eighteen. Annie's parents were definitely cooler and more laid back about stuff like that. Anyway, that's how she looked in the old world, so Amelia was happy to see that that's how she looked in the new one too.

They went off biking like they normally did down the bike path, past the park and the tennis courts, and then down to the mall for a bit. There was nobody hanging out outside the mall, so they decided to head back because it was getting dark. They talked and laughed, and Amelia asked Annie questions about all of their classmates and anything she could think of to get more information about this new, more stable world of hers.

Annie on the other hand, found it strange that her best friend was asking her questions that she should've already known the answers too. "Why are you asking me all this stuff?" she asked. However, Annie was like a dog that sees a squirrel and just has to run after it, very easily distracted. All Amelia had to do was start talking about a tattoo that she would love to have when she gets older, and Annie forgot all about those questions and started bragging that her mom was letting her get a tattoo when she turns sixteen.

They rode home quickly because the sun was going down. They got to Amelia's driveway first, said goodbye and Amelia watched as Annie rode her bike down the street a few houses and into her driveway. Amelia parked her bike in the garage and went into the house through the garage door.

She hung up her helmet and took off her shoes as usual. That warm and peaceful sense of calm came over her again as she walked into the house.

It didn't take her long to embrace this new life and to feel like she belonged, which felt amazing to her because Amelia had never felt like she belonged anywhere in her entire life. There was never any time and she always felt afraid of getting too comfortable and making connections with people that she would always have to leave again.

It felt really good to know that she would be here, and that she could continue making friends, maybe even make Brendan, her 'almost' boyfriend, her actual boyfriend, and really start caring about him without worrying that she would have to leave.

As shocking as today had been, she was looking forward to seeing what tomorrow would be like. She hugged her parents goodnight like she always did. Her mom even smelled the same and her dad kissed her on the cheek as usual. But before she went up to bed, she stopped and asked her parents, "Do you guys ever plan on moving to a new place?"

Her parents looked at each other and answered, "No, not at all. Why would we want to leave such a nice place?"

She walked up the stairs to bed still wondering how this could have happened but trying to tell herself to enjoy the calmness of the moment and that everything would be ok. She crawled into her bed, fell fast asleep and dreamed of Brendan Walsh until the next morning, as usual.

*

THE NEXT DAY, AMELIA WOKE TO A BRAND-NEW DAY WITHOUT dread, or worry or a sense of uncertainty. She was secure in the knowledge that she would be here for quite a while and she could actually start planning her days, weeks and months. It was a great feeling and she smiled from ear to ear as she walked down the stairs.

The smell of breakfast was cooking as usual. Dad in his military uniform, was drinking his coffee, and mom was still in her bathrobe buttering toast. She smiled and said good morning to Amelia and asked how she wanted her eggs today. Amelia's mom always said that breakfast was the most important meal of the day and insisted on her eating a hearty one.

"Mom, I can't wait to get to school today, so I really have to go!" she yelled running to the door.

"STOP!" Amelia's dad yelled, and Amelia stopped dead in her tracks, shocked that her had dad yelled at her that way.

She turned around slowly with her eyes wide and her Mom smiled and said, "Eat your breakfast, dear."

She sat down and ate her breakfast quickly and all the while those words echoed back in Amelia's head and cut into her brain like a knife.

Okay, that was weird! she said to herself, but she continued down the street to pick up Annie. As she walked, she looked around at the street, the houses, the cars, and everything was just like she remembered it. Just then, Annie came out from her driveway still looking as weird as ever. Annie smiled and waved and thought how great it was to have her best friend here with her.

They walked to school quickly and when Amelia got there, she looked so hard for something to be wrong, but it was all the same here, too! She recognized all of the other students, she saw her teachers and they recognized her and said hi as usual. She roamed the halls and found that her classes were all in the same rooms, and best of all, she found her locker which she was happy to discover, was still beside Brendan Walsh's!

Amelia spotted Brendan down the hall and when she called his name and waved, he turned his head and looked at her as if to say, *who are you, go away*. She was stunned and Annie was too. They continued walking down the hall to their homeroom class and Amelia saw her basketball coach. She ran up to him and said, "Hey coach, I'm ready for the big game today!"

The coach stared at her with a confused look and laughed, "Hi Amelia, that's good, are you offering to help on the sidelines? We could sure use the extra help! Thanks!" And the coach walked away. The look on Amelia's face was of sheer panic and confusion. The sight of Brendan walking away from her would be etched in her mind all day. The words that the coach said would be etched in her mind too. The sight of Amelia's sad face would also be etched in Annie's mind all day.

Amelia got through the day, but just couldn't figure out what was going on. How could so many things be the same, but yet the biggest things in her life be so off? She and Brendan were almost an item in the school; they were both basketball champions, and were very popular. This was a nightmare! The other students usually smiled and yelled hi to Amelia as she strutted through the school like she owned it, but now they hardly noticed her. "This isn't right," she whispered under her breath, and then she remembered her mom and dad this morning. Her dad had yelled at her but he had never yelled before; and those words that her mom had said, such a little thing, but she had never called her dear ever before. "Something's not right," she whispered again.

Can I tell Annie what's going on? Amelia wondered. She pretended all day not to be totally blown away by the no Brendan and no basketball discoveries. Suddenly, something made her remember what was missing in her room as she thought about the basketball game. *My trophies weren't in my room, that's what was missing last night!*

She had to find out where she was, and how she ended up in this strange place. What was going on? Where were her other parents? Did they just disappear? Are they out there somewhere frantic with worry about her or did she even exist in that world? All of these questions came crashing down on her at once.

"Amelia, Amelia! Can you hear me?" Annie yelled.

"Oh sorry, what did you say?" asked Amelia.

"You were so out of it! You look like you've seen a ghost! Are you Okay?" Annie asked, looking worried.

"Yes, I-I'm just really tired and need to get home, sorry."

Annie watched as Amelia bolted down the street. She knew that something was wrong with her best friend, and it tore her apart. She had to figure out what she could do to fix this situation. "I've gotta help her," she whispered under her breath. "It's just not right." And she walked the rest of the way home alone.

Annie tossed and turned for hours that night, and just couldn't forget about how sad Amelia was. *It's as if she's physically here, but not mentally here,* she thought. And those questions she was asking last night about things she should already know the answers to? *What's going on?* she wondered. *Something's not right.* All of these questions just kept nagging at her so much that she just had to talk to her friend before the morning. *I've got to do something!*

Annie snuck out of her bedroom window, as she had been known to do before, and she ran down the street to Amelia's house. She noticed the light on in her bedroom, so she took out her phone and just as she began to text Amelia, she spotted the light on in her basement window. Strangely, she heard a familiar sound. A soft, spa-like music was playing down there. *That's weird,* thought Annie, *it's like 12:30 at night.* She moved quietly towards the window as if the music was drawing her there. She bent down and looked into the basement.

She saw Amelia's parents talking and almost arguing with each other. She couldn't hear what they were saying, but then suddenly Amelia's mom grabbed at her face and started pulling at it! Then came the body, the arms, then the legs, like she was pulling herself out of a really tight wetsuit, but it wasn't a wetsuit, it was her skin! And as she pulled herself out of it, Annie could see a two armed, two legged being that was definitely not from this planet! The being looked humanoid in physical structure, but had a very different face than a human's face, and she had very large hands and feet too! The skin was a washed-out beige colour and the eyes were red. The creature turned and opened what looked like a metal briefcase. Inside the briefcase was a glowing, dome shaped thing that seemed to pulse with energy like a heartbeat. She touched it for a long time and Annie kept watching until the creature's skin became a beautiful greenish blue colour.

Next, she saw Amelia's dad do exactly the same thing. He pulled at his human looking skin and climbed out of the body he was in and touched the dome with his beige-gray hands and then his colour changed to an even brighter hue of turquoise with flecks of yellows, and pinks and purples. It was just beautiful! Annie saw the energy go into his body and both creatures seemed to be happy and revived.

Annie didn't know what to do, but she knew she had to tell Amelia, but how? She couldn't let Amelia know the truth! Annie decided to text

Amelia to come outside and meet her and she would pretend to confront her. She grabbed a big stick to make it look real, and as Amelia came out the back door, Annie charged at her and yelled, "Stop right there or I'll hit you!"

Amelia was shocked and didn't know what was going on. "What the hell?" she screamed, "Annie, what are you doing?"

Annie yelled back, "Who are you and where are you from, and what have you done with my friend Amelia?"

"I'm Amelia, Annie, it's me!" Amelia yelled.

"How do I know that? Your parents aren't humans and they have really strange skin and faces and a glowing dome that gives off energy and-"

"Whoa," screamed Amelia, "Slow down, are you sleepwalking or something?"

Once Annie realized that Amelia really had no clue, she put the stick down, took a deep breath and tried to explain why she came over to talk to her so late at night. "I'm so sorry Amelia! Your parents are not your parents, this whole situation is so messed up, and I just wanted you to know that-"

"I know what you're gonna say," interrupted Amelia.

"You do?" asked Annie.

"Yes, something very weird is going on, and I was planning to tell you, but I just didn't want you to think I was crazy."

"So, you know about this and you're okay with it?" Annie asked.

"Yes, well kind of, it was my choice, but now I'm not so sure and-"

"Amelia, there's a lot more to this story that you don't know!" interrupted Annie, "Come on, I have to let you see for yourself!" and she grabbed Amelia's hand and pulled her to the basement window. Amelia looked in and saw them. They were still there, touching this glowing dome like object in a metal case and their bodies were kind of glowing too as if they were being energized by this thing. Amelia was shocked and wanted to look away but couldn't. They were quite beautiful to look at with their bright, sparkling skin. She was entranced by their appearance and she suddenly began to hear music playing. She recognized the music and snapped out of her trance.

"Oh my God! That's the music I heard yesterday!" She looked at Annie, then back to the basement. Then suddenly the music disappeared and her parents, well, the things, were no longer in the basement!

Amelia shook with fear and tears began to flow down her face. Annie threw her arms around Amelia and told her that it would all be okay, but how could it? With her real parents gone, and these aliens having taken over! "Why are you so calm? Aren't you freaking out too?"

"One of us has to stay calm and think about a plan," said Annie. Amelia grabbed Annie's shoulders and shook her as she cried. "Annie, I'm so scared! Who, what are those things? Where are they now? Are all of those people out there like them? I have to get back over the hedge to the world I came from, but I don't know if I'll ever be able to! I was so stupid to choose this world! Will you help me Annie, for both our sakes?"

After a long pause, Annie said, "Yes I will, I came over here to help you and that's what I'm going to do! Now let's make a plan before it's too late."

*

THE MORNING CAME FAST AS THEY PLANNED THEIR NEXT MOVE and before they knew it, they were racing back to their bedrooms before their 'parents' knew they were gone. Their plan was to fake illness and have the day to do some exploration in Amelia's basement while all of their 'parents' were at work.

It worked since they didn't sleep the night before, they both looked so tired and rundown that their parents agreed to let them stay home from school. Once both sets of 'parents' were gone, they texted each other and agreed to meet in their secret spot behind the shed in Annie's backyard. This spot was the same as it was in the other world and it was a great spot to hide and talk about their secrets, to gossip and today, talk about the first part of their plan to figure out what to do.

"Let's make a chart," said Amelia, "On one side we'll write what we know and on the other side we'll write what we don't know."

"Great idea!" said Annie, and she drew the chart.

"What we know is that my parents are definitely NOT human but are pretending to be human and be my parents. They are also doing a great job at that, except for the slip calling me 'dear'. Mom has never called me dear, and the way dad yelled at me was crazy! We know that they seem to get energy from that glowing thing, so they must be creatures who feed off that kind of energy. What we don't know is what kind of energy it is, and what else it's powering. I also know that I can leave the house and the yard and the world outside is pretty much the same except for the Brendan and basketball issues, so that's a big clue that the creatures messed up somewhere along the line."

Annie knew Amelia was right. There was a big mess up and she just lowered her head in disbelief.

"What's that look for?" Amelia asked Annie. "You're the one who said to stay calm, so we could think about a plan. Now you look freaked. I need you to help me, Annie!"

Annie's wits came back to her as she shook her head. "Another thing we don't know," added Annie, "is why they're doing this, and if the people in the town are the real people who are being controlled somehow or if they're aliens too. And why am I not being controlled like them? What's that case with the glowing dome? Is it some kind of power source that's allowing this alternate world to exist?"

There were too many questions, and it made their heads spin. So, off they went to Amelia's basement to find the metal case. They searched and searched for it but couldn't find it anywhere. Then they suddenly heard the music that was playing last night, and they stopped. Where was it coming from? They walked in slow, synchronized steps around the basement listening for the low, enchanting tune to get louder as they got closer to it.

Annie called, "Here!" It was under an old pile of firewood and they quickly took it out. It was hot to touch, and Annie dropped it fast, "AAAGH!" she yelled. When it hit the concrete floor, the case split open and they saw the glowing dome and felt the heat all around them. The music was playing, and the glowing thing mesmerized them for a few seconds.

Amelia suddenly had an image of herself walking back through the hedge, and she ran outside. Annie ran after her. "That's where I came through," she said, "but there's no opening! I have to go, I have to try!" So she ran towards the hedge and as she got closer, she reached out to touch it.

"Amelia! NO!" screamed Annie. Amelia shot back like a ragdoll and crashed a few feet away on her back. She got the biggest shock of her life and was knocked unconscious for a few seconds. Annie saw the whole thing happen and she thought Amelia was dead. "Amelia!" she called out to her and when she got to her, she was relieved to see Amelia opening her eyes and moving! "Are you okay?" Annie yelled.

"Yeah, I-I th-think so," Amelia stuttered.

"That thing in the case is a very strong source of power," cried Annie, "you shouldn't have touched the hedge like that!"

Suddenly, Amelia's mom was there and she asked in a calm voice, "What are you girls doing, dear?"

They had to think fast!

"Nothing mom, I was running and twisted my ankle."

"Well, we'd better get some ice on it, dear," her mom said, almost robot-like.

"Sure, mom," she said as she motioned to Annie with her eyes. Annie knew that Amelia meant for her to go down and try to break the source of that power, but how? She had no idea. Amelia kept her 'mom' busy getting the ice, asking for a snack and talking about her day.

Annie snuck down to the basement and saw that the case was still open and glowing. She didn't want to touch it, but then she saw some buttons on it that could be the controls. She found some thick work gloves and put them on and picked up the case. She started banging on the buttons randomly and quickly until suddenly the glowing stopped, and the heat subsided. "Oh wow!" She couldn't believe she did it. *Maybe that means that the hedge isn't electrified anymore!* she thought excitedly.

Annie carefully put the case down and ran up into the kitchen and motioned to Amelia that she got it with a thumbs up. Amelia told her 'mom' that she and Annie would go outside to sit on the porch, and she pretended to limp out and Annie pretended to help her walk. "I got the thing turned off, I think. It's not glowing and hot anymore. We have to get out there quick!" Annie whispered to Amelia.

Amelia's mom turned and said, "Be careful, dear," and that was the last straw for Amelia.

"Stop calling me dear, I'm not your dear, and you're not my Mom! You're a creature pretending to be my Mom! What have you done to me and to my real parents!?" Amelia screamed.

Annie looked pleadingly into Amelia's mom's eyes and she dragged Amelia out of the house. Amelia's mom raised her hand and a hot streak of what looked like lightning shot out and towards Amelia. Annie jumped in front of Amelia, raised her hand and a shot of electricity bolted across the air to block it.

Amelia couldn't believe her eyes! "What the hell are you?" she yelled.

"I'm your best friend and I'm trying to help you, so stay beside me if you want to get through that opening!" They both looked up and saw the opening. She continued to help her friend get to the hedge opening, and Amelia decided to listen to her.

They were getting closer as Amelia's dad appeared in the backyard. "STOP!" he yelled, but this time she didn't. He ran after them. He was more powerful than the female creature, and Annie knew this. She saw his red eyes and knew what that meant, and as he raised his hand to shoot a powerful bolt at Amelia, Annie challenged him. She was a female but was younger, which meant that she didn't need to re-charge as often as the adult creatures. This knowledge was the power that Annie needed. She once again jumped in front of her friend, and with quick hands, was the first to shoot. The creature shot a blocking bolt with his hand and the two bolts of power collided in the air above them. Amelia at this point had stopped running, and was just watching the whole thing with her eyes wide with disbelief.

The male creature got up and began to run, and again, Annie held out her hand to shoot at him. He was losing his speed and agility because he needed more power, and she was able to use this to her advantage and make contact with his body. He shot backwards.

She was a young female, so her jolts weren't that powerful, but they were powerful enough against one who was in a weakened state. This was a good thing for now. The male was stunned, but moving a little, and then Amelia noticed her mom running the other way.

"Annie, the other one!" she screamed. Amelia's 'mom' ran down towards the basement and they knew that she was going to try to turn that thing back on. They knew they had no time to waste! They couldn't let that opening disappear!

The male creature was still down, but trying to get up, so Annie knew what she had to do.

She ran towards Amelia and with one swift push, Amelia was through the opening. Annie yelled, "I'm sorry, I'll miss you!" to Amelia as she pushed her through.

Amelia yelled, "Thank you!" to Annie, but it was too late. Amelia was through the hedge so fast that Annie never heard her.

Annie watched her go to the other side and disappear, and sadness gripped her. *Goodbye my friend!* she thought to herself. Annie didn't know what it was like to have a friend until Amelia came along. She was Annie's one true friend and she would've done anything for her.

She watched the opening close up which meant that the power was once again being controlled.

She looked over at the human looking man lying on the ground. She ran over to him and helped him up. He was heavy and so weak by this point, but she managed to get him down the stairs into the basement. The female ran over to help as best she could. She was also very weak by this point. The creatures looked at Annie with confusion in their eyes, and she looked at them with anger because they could've really hurt Amelia!

Annie helped them get out of their human "skin" and get their hands on the dome, then she stepped back and began to pull off her human self and exposed her beige-gray skin tone and red eyes. She too was almost out of energy from all of the events of the day with Amelia. She touched the glowing dome for a long time and her skin finally began to turn a beautiful blue-green hue just like her parents' skin.

She appreciated their help with Amelia more than they knew, but everything just went so very wrong! The two girls were both so sad about Amelia having to leave that Annie decided to take matters into her own hands and try to make things better.

"How could I have been so wrong?" she thought. "I totally underestimated the power that our alien race has over these humans and Amelia could've been really hurt or worse, and it would've been all my fault!"

While the glowing dome brought the life back into the three creatures, Annie thought about how lucky she was to have known Amelia, and she smiled because in the end she knew she did the right thing to let her go.

*

AMELIA LOOKED DOWN FROM THE AIRPLANE. Her parents were beside her on their way to another adventure in a whole new city. She would never forget the last two days and she still wondered in disbelief about how it all happened, and what it all meant. She tried texting Annie a dozen times, but there was no response. She needed answers and needed to know if Annie was okay. Then, Amelia's dad said that the airplane was just going over their old neighbourhood, so she looked out the small window to try to see it.

She looked down and thought she saw a colourful glow radiating up through the wispy clouds, and she smiled.

Diary of a Madwoman

By Janet Edwards

SUNDAY, MAY 6TH:

I'm so happy. This could be the one. I met a wonderful man named
Daniel at Tina's birthday dinner last night. He wasn't supposed to be there,
and neither was I to be honest. I had such a hard week at work, (hilarious
to say a 'hard week' because I do nothing more than data entry). Yet every
day, my boss seemed to be on a tirade at everyone and every little thing, and
it got me down. I was looking forward to a quiet weekend in front of the
TV and didn't feel up to facing a crowd of people. Tina convinced me at the
last minute to get out. She said it's good for me to socialize when I'm feeling

down and not to stay cooped up on my own. I'm so glad she did or I wouldn't have met Daniel. He is so handsome - blonde hair and the bluest eyes I have ever seen. Dark blue, almost like sapphire's. He said he works in IT, but I can't remember the company name. And funny enough, it was a work function that should have kept him away from Tina's dinner, but he decided to switch his plans at the last minute. Tina's boyfriend invited him. (Who knew Jack had such good-looking friends!). We laughed so much together, he seemed really into me. We exchanged numbers and he said he'll call me after work tomorrow. I'm thrilled. Except now I'll have to come up with things to talk about that are interesting over the phone. I'm so much better in person. I know I'm funny and I love to see people's faces when I make them laugh. Even still, it'll be wonderful to talk to him again. He's so cool, and very smart. I got a different vibe from him, not at all like when I met Finn, or even Max for that matter. No, Daniel is different. He and I were on the same page with so many things. We like alot of the same bands, we've watched a bunch of the same shows on Netflix. I gave him a few suggestions for things to watch next and he said he would check them out. I wish I could remember his company's name. It wasn't listed on his Facebook page or anywhere on his Instagram. I scrolled all the way to almost the beginning of his socials to get a glimpse of his life, and to get ideas on what to talk about tomorrow - things that will interest him, (totally on the sly, of course, I don't want him to think I'm a stalker!). He's into fishing, camping, and loves the Detroit Red Wings. Lots of photos with guy friends at social events. And a dog, oh how I love a man with a dog. His life seems so interesting. How exciting to possibly become a part of it now. I can already imagine all the cute photos we'll post together, doing all kinds of fun and wonderful things! I feel like a giddy teenager again. There was this blonde though that kept popping up in photos over the course of a year...I wonder if she's an ex? She's really beautiful. Almost as tall as he is, long hair, long legs. The kind of beauty that makes someone like me feel insecure. Though it was never mentioned in any of the posts that it was a girlfriend, so maybe she's just a close friend. Although, men don't have beautiful women like that around for platonic friendship. She must be an ex. Ugh, this is stupid, and I'm getting myself all worked up. He was into *me* last night, he wanted to talk to *me* and he took *my* phone number. I'm sure that blonde is history. This could be something special, me and him. I can't wait until tomorrow night.

MONDAY, MAY 7TH:

It's 8 o'clock in the evening, no call from Daniel yet. Perhaps he had to work a bit late today. I don't recall him mentioning what time he finishes work, or what his schedule is like so this could be normal. I shouldn't have expected him to call the moment he walked in the door. I'm sure he had things to do. I wonder if he's okay? I certainly hope he didn't forget that he told me he'd call. I wonder if I should call him? I'll wait until around 9 o'clock if I haven't heard anything. But then again, maybe I shouldn't push. I don't want to bother him. And who knows, someone could have stopped by his house unannounced and he's been tied up with them. I hate when people do that to me. I'll give it a bit more time. I don't want to seem desperate. He said he would call me tonight - Monday night after work - that's what he said. It's Monday night after work and he'll call. I checked his Instagram and he hasn't posted anything new, so there's no indication that he's doing something else tonight. We made such a connection with each other on Saturday, there's no way he won't call. I'm sure he's just busy.

Maybe he's cleaning up from supper right now. Or maybe he squeezed in a workout - he definitely looks like the type. He'll call any minute, I know it. This extra time is at least allowing me to think of more things to talk about. I realized I didn't say much about myself - about my job, or my family. Not that there's much to say. I'll end up having to exaggerate to sound interesting. I'm sure I can come up with a few funny anecdotes to make the call fun for him. We talked mostly about him Saturday night, and about music we like, concerts we'd still like to go to. Tonight I'll tell him all about me. He mentioned that he travelled to Italy a couple of years back, (he thought of it when we both ordered the same Italian red with dinner). I'll have to remember to ask him about that trip. Men like to talk about themselves, at least I know that. Funny, there were no pictures of Italy on his social media, which is a bit strange. Could it have been a trip with the mystery blonde and he's blocked those photos? Or took them down because she was in them? I'll just casually ask him who he travelled with and get the story out of him. I wonder if it's too soon to ask him to be my date to Simone's wedding in August? Or to come camping with me over the long weekend, now that I know he's into camping. He'd probably be floored that I asked him to do something that's right up his alley. I've been daydreaming non-stop about him since Saturday night. About being the woman on his arm. The one he shares all his intimate secrets with. The one he vents to after a bad day at the office. I wonder what his parents are like, and if he has brothers and sisters. I can't wait to meet them all. The family dinners we'll share together will be so much fun. Oh, please call soon!

*

HEADING TO BED NOW, IT'S 10:30 PM. He didn't call. I thought about sending a quick text but decided against it. I don't want to be pushy. It's nice to be pursued, and after all, he did say he would call me. I should just be patient, I'm sure I'll hear from him. I hope nothing bad has happened.

TUESDAY, MAY 8TH:

Still no call from Daniel. I don't understand what's going on. We met three days ago and he should have called by now. Have I done something wrong? I must have said something that offended him. I've been wracking my brain trying to think of what I could have said, or could have done that turned him off. Maybe I shouldn't have said anything about being single for so long, and that I've only been 'casually dating'. That could have raised a red flag for him. He may think there's something wrong with me, like I'm a complete flake and can't hold a man. Or perhaps I shouldn't have had that second glass of wine. I can get a bit giggly after two. Oh, What did I do? Why hasn't he called me? I don't understand how two people can meet, hit it off, have such an amazing connection with each other and all those proverbial sparks fly like mad and then - nothing. Why do men always go silent? I'm tired of it. If you say you're going to call a person, then call! Why is it so bloody difficult? I must have done something, there must have been something in my tone, or something about my body language that gave him the impression I wasn't interested. I always do this. I always think I'm doing well and things are finally going to go my way and then bang! The universe turns against me. I bet I know what happened. He mentioned his last relationship had ended badly a couple of years ago, (probably that goddman blonde he went to Italy with). Something about her pushing too hard for marriage and kids and he wasn't ready...and I'm pretty sure I made a comment about it being for the best that he got out of it, and that he shouldn't be pressured into things like that. I bet that did it. I bet that's what turned him off of me. He's probably not over her. He's probably still grieving the relationship and I went and told him he's better off. Why do I always put my foot in my mouth like that? I can never seem to keep my opinions to myself. I think I'm being helpful, or saying what I believe people need to hear to feel better, but obviously I don't know what I'm talking about. One thing that's rolling around in my head, which makes me so sad, is that maybe it's possible I got it all wrong. Maybe he wasn't into me at all. He was just humouring me by asking for my number so I wouldn't feel so pathetic. He felt sorry for me because I was there alone. Well fuck him, he was there alone too! He's not better than me. I went to that dinner for Tina and to celebrate her birthday, not for him. I don't care about him - I don't even *know* him! I just bet too that his phone is literally right beside him, right now. No one goes anywhere without their phones these days. It takes mere seconds to send a text, and a few minutes to check in and say hello. What the hell is his problem? I can't believe how fucking rude he's being to me. I don't deserve this. No one deserves this kind of treatment, it's awful. I'm so angry. I'm fed up with men like him thinking they can treat a woman like this. To say they're going to do something and then don't. To trick you into believing them to be a certain way, to think they like you and want to get to know you. They pretend to be interested in what you're saying and then disappear into thin air. I don't understand any of this. I don't understand how someone can be so cruel. That blonde had a lucky escape.

I bet he treated her like this too, with no regard for her feelings. She's lucky she didn't marry someone as inconsiderate as him. Well, I've made a decision. I'm done with him. If he ever does call, I'm not answering. It'll ring and ring and he can wonder and worry about where I am and why I've gone quiet. He can get a taste of this for himself, and feel sick to his stomach like I do right now. And maybe, just maybe, he'll think twice about treating the next woman he meets this way. What a horrible man. I hope he has bad luck in love from here on out. I wish him nothing but grief for the rest of his miserable fucking days. I won't fall for this again.

WEDNESDAY, MAY 9TH:

I can't get out of bed this morning. I feel so dejected. I can barely lift my head off my pillow. Any energy I had has drained from my entire body. I called in sick to work, I don't have it in me to face anybody today. I'm not up for it and there's no way I'll be able to fake a smile. Not today. Why does this keep happening to me? I get my hopes up and people constantly disappoint. It's getting so hard to keep living like this, in a world that is so miserable. The anxiety of it all turns my stomach into knots. I'm alone. I feel so...heavy, so exhausted, like I'm drowning. My mind hurts, is that possible? For someone's mind to hurt? I've been crying all night, I didn't sleep much. I haven't looked at myself in the mirror yet, but I can feel the grief all over my face. I'm so tired of giving and giving, of getting excited at the prospect of something great happening, and it never does. Envisioning my life turning out a certain way, but it doesn't. It's like I'm never going to get this right. And the worst part is that I know I deserve it. I know I'm not a good person. I've done so many stupid things, said so many terrible things to people in my past that I'm sure this is karma coming back to get me now. I haven't always been the nicest girlfriend to past loves and now I'm being punished for it. These wonderful men are being dangled in front of me then ripped away. I don't deserve them. I'm worthless, unlovable. Daniel didn't call because I'm not good enough for a man like that. I don't have an incredible job or an incredible life. I don't have anything going for me that would keep a man like that interested. I'm not special. I muddle through the days with fake enthusiasm for people I don't like being around at a job I don't like going to. I have no hobbies that make me unique, no aspirations for the future. No motivation to change myself, to improve things that need improving. I don't look forward to things anymore. All of my tomorrows look bleak, empty. And the few times I do get excited about someone or something, it gets proven to me over and over that I'm not good enough. I'm simply no good for a great life. What would a man like Daniel ever gain by dating someone like me? I have nothing to offer. Here I am, 37-years old, never married, no children. A common data entry clerk with no degree to further myself. I live in a tiny apartment with my tiny cat. In my tiny bed. I have no savings, no car. I've bounced from job to job, home to home. It's humiliating how I can't settle. I'm sure my friends think I'm pitiful. I know I am. I don't even have beauty going for me. I'm plain, with muddy eyes and a crooked smile. I'm sure I pale in comparison to every woman Daniel has ever known. I should be relieved he didn't call me, for his sake. I think he has saved himself from a world of misery. Now he never has to find out how dull I am. How I'm not worthy of love from a great man. He escaped a project that needs so much fixing. I'm a failure. I've failed at everything I've ever touched. Who the hell would want to get mixed up with someone like me?

THURSDAY, MAY 10TH:

Daniel called! He's taking me to see The Killers on Saturday night. He said he'd been waiting to make sure he could get the tickets before calling so he could surprise me. How wonderful of him. I knew he was special.

I'm so happy. This could be the one...

The Space Between

By A . R . Finley

THUNDER CRACKED THE SILENCE

Startled, Suzie turned her attention from the door to the window. She stared out into the darkness and the darkness stared back. Black clouds raged and swirled in unsettling patterns as the elements battled for position. Another boom rang out. Lightning streaked the sky as the clouds ripped open and unleashed their wrath of torrents on the ground below. Sheets of water crashed against the windowpane and drummed an unnatural rhythm. The hair on her arms stood on end.

Her stomach clenched harder as she tore her gaze from the window and focused back on the door. From beneath it, the tiny crack betrayed her, and the dark crept in. A thousand tiny tentacles stretched across the hardwood floor, getting ever closer to her metal bedframe. She cinched her legs to her chest as far as she could and pressed her back against the headboard. The cold metal sent shivers down her spine. Unable to scream for help, unable to muster the courage to jump off her bed and escape, she watched in despair.

Mo... m... The words formed in her mouth, but no sound emerged.

Worm-like icicles gnawed at her foot and slid between her toes. She pleaded with herself to move, to yell, to make noise of some sort, but to no avail. They clawed at her ankle and snaked around her leg, spiraling up towards her body. Cold emanated from the unearthly lassos and seared frostbite into her flesh. Tears began to flow as she writhed in agony.

"MOMMY!" she finally managed.

The shadows recoiled in a smoky haze. They flitted up above her, one shadow merging into another, the mass twitching and morphing, until a creature emerged. Its two red orbs eyed her intently as it lowered its head to meet hers. Lava-hot drool dripped from between its cracked lips, landed on her cheek, and burned her skin. She squirmed as it forced its serpent-like tongue deep down her throat. With reckless abandon, its barbed tail sliced through the air, as the beast extracted her soul.

*

ONE FINAL CLAP OF THUNDER RUMBLED ACROSS THE SKY. In its wake, it shook the house, and forced Megan from her slumber. Through squinted eyes, she looked around the room for the source of the noise. Water droplets, remnants of the storm, clung to the window, and confirmed that a storm had passed through. She clenched at her chest and checked for her necklace, a reflex from her childhood, before rolling over to resume her sleep.

Sleep did not come. In a state of unease, she turned on her back and opened her eyes. Out of the darkness, from inches above, two red eyes leered at her. Frozen in fear, a knot formed in her stomach. A bead of molten liquid rolled down her neck and singed the collar of her nightgown. The rancid stench of rotted flesh permeated the air. She willed herself to reach for the lamp and pulled the bead chain. Light illuminated the room and the vision vanished. After shaking off the experience, she grabbed her cell phone and headed down the hallway to check on Suzie.

The door creaked open. Once inside, Megan turned on the flashlight app and scanned the room. Suzie laid askew on her bed. One arm slumped on the floor. Her heart jumped into her throat. She threw the overhead lights on and scrambled to her bed.

"Suzie!" She shook her. "Suzie! Wake up!"

Suzie lay unresponsive. Megan pressed her fingers against her neck and checked for a pulse. A weak heartbeat tapped back. She unlocked her phone and dialed 9-1-1. The call stalled and the line disconnected. After several failed connection attempts, she scooped her up in her arms and rushed her to the car. Still haunted by the vision of the red orbs, fresh in her mind, she revved the engine and peeled out of the driveway, the car fishtailing on the slick asphalt.

*

PANIC GRIPPED THE EMERGENCY ROOM. Parent after parent arrived, unconscious children limp in their arms. Clad in blue, head nurse Jean rushed from one patient to the next and triaged the queue. Megan held Suzie close to her chest and waited her turn. The fluorescent lights hummed, as if speaking to her directly, relaying their own tale of woe, and blocked out the pleas of despair around her.

"Megan?"

Megan jumped to her feet, Suzie snug in her arms. "Yes!"

"Please come with me," said Jean.

They snaked through the network of hallways. Little purple horseshoes, painted on the floor, led the way. The beds in each room they passed filled with comatose children. Tubes and cords stretched from machines and poles to their tiny bodies. At the end of the corridor, Jean stopped and motioned Megan into a room.

"Please wait here. Dr. Xavier will see you in a moment."

"Thank you."

Megan slid into the room. Six beds, three on either side, all unoccupied, lined the room. Cloth curtains, shields of false hope, hung heavy between the beds. She rushed to the stretcher in the left corner, close to the window, and placed Suzie on the bed. Outside, the storm illuminated the sky one town over.

As the doctor entered the room, Megan pounced on him. "I woke up after the storm and found her like this. She won't wake up! Please –"

The doctor held up his hand. "Take a deep breath, Mom. Let me examine her."

Suzie's pulse remained weak. The bright red burn on her cheek oozed as he brushed his finger across the wound. Bluish-white striations spread across her foot, up her calf, and disappeared under the cuff of her pajamas. Her pupils, pinpricks of black, unresponsive to any stimuli. Concern and confusion etched across his face as he entered the data on her chart.

Megan broke the silence. "What's wrong with her?"

"I... I don't know."

"What? What do you mean!?"

"All night long parents have been bringing in their children in this exact same state. The only difference I've seen so far is the mark on her cheek. Do you know when she got that?"

She shook her head, her eyes wide in disbelief.

"We are going to clean up her wounds, give her an intravenous line, and set up some monitors. Why don't you take a walk and try to clear your head?"

Jean brought the next patient into the room and motioned to the bed closest to the door. After getting instructions from the doctor, she made her way to Suzie's bed, nodded her head in Megan's direction, and drew the faded yellow curtain closed. Megan stepped out into the hallway.

*

DESPERATION HUNG HEAVY IN THE AIR. After five days, not one child recovered, no sign of change observed. Megan torqued her body out of the visitor's chair next to Suzie's bed and stretched her arms high above her head. Pins and needles ambushed her feet as she stood up and the circulation returned. She made her way outside the room and headed for the chapel.

Megan eyed the third pew as the chapel door swung shut behind her. The oaken support, unforgiving and cold, gave her an odd sense of comfort. At two in the afternoon, she had the chapel to herself. She folded her hands and bowed her head to pray.

*

"HELLO. I'M ANNABELLE."

Startled, Megan jerked upright. Next to her, an elderly lady held out her bony hand. Her wiry grey hair, lit from behind, framed her face like an ominous aura. One eye, solid white, the other pale blue, stared at her in anticipation.

"Hello. I'm Megan."

She offered her hand. Annabelle grabbed it with an impossible strength, flipped her arm palm-side up, and pushed up the sleeve of her cardigan.

"As I thought."

Megan squirmed her hand out of Annabelle's grip.

"What are you doing?"

"I needed to know."

"Know what?"

"You bear the mark."

Uncertain how to respond, Megan eyed Annabelle with skepticism, ready to bolt.

"Please hear me out. There's not much time left. The Great White Spot is waning. Every thirty years a storm brews on Saturn. This creates a rift across the universe. On earth, a fissure that allows the beast to easily pass from dark into light. It captures the souls of the children to feast upon until the next storm. The crevasse is closing and with it your chance to free the children."

Megan's mouth dropped open. Her brain reeled. She had enough concerns without listening to the ravings of a mad woman. She stood up to leave.

"I know you've seen its eyes. Somewhere, in the darkness. Those two red orbs. Hypnotic. Terrifying. They don't just *look* at you. They penetrate deep into your soul."

As Megan sank back onto the pew, Annabelle continued.

"Only children can see the beast. Only adults who were marked as a child can see the beast. That scar on your arm. It's a burn from its saliva. That is what connects you to it. You escaped it once. You can do it again. You just need to remember how."

Megan swallowed hard. "I've been having visions. Nightmares? I'm not sure which. Every time I see those eyes, they draw me in further. But I don't know how to defeat it. How can I bring those memories back? How do I remember?"

Annabelle lowered her head and took a deep breath. She took Megan's hands in hers and locked eyes with her before continuing. "The only way to remember is to go back. Back to the space between. That is where the children are. That is where you can save them."

"What is the space between?"

"It's the space between light and dark. Beasts cannot survive in the light. Just as we cannot survive in the dark. The space between lies within the two extremes. It's the place where shadows take form and creatures materialize. A place where both man and beast are vulnerable."

"Yes! Okay! I will do anything to get my daughter back. How do I get there?"

"You need to follow the shadows of the shadows. Just don't lose track of the light. That is your way back."

*

DARKNESS DEVOURED THE LAST RAYS OF DAYLIGHT. Megan slammed the car door shut and rushed into the house. She ran up the stairs, threw herself on her bed, and let her eyes adjust to the dark. Out of the corner of her eye, a shadow squiggled towards the baseboard and disappeared into the corner. She waited.

Hot air wafted across her forehead, the foul odour of the beast unmistakable. She resisted the urge to look at it directly. By her hand, a shadow pulsated and exploded, spawning into thousands of maggot-like shadows. Each one wriggled over her hand and up her sleeve. Its barbed tail slammed down on the bed and poked a hole through the mattress. Angered by the lack of a response, the beast released a high-pitched shriek before it scrambled away.

Its claws scraped along the floor, gouging razor-thin grooves into the hardwood. As the last of it slithered under the door, she saw it. The shadow of the shadow. The shadow of the beast. She hopped off the bed and chased after it. Down the stairs, out the back door, and towards the well.

Each step grew more cumbersome than the last. The ground still saturated from the recent storm. Grass gave way to mud that clung to her shoes and pulled her further down below the surface, deeper and deeper. As she sunk further into the earth her breathing labored until everything faded to black.

*

A SLICE OF LIGHT FROM FAR ABOVE CAST A DIM GLOW THROUGHOUT THE underground cavern and met her eyes as she pried them open. Beneath her the cold rock pushed hard against her spine. The air, stagnant and moist, burned her lungs as she struggled to breathe. She picked herself up off the floor and squinted as she looked around her.

In front of her, cast in black shadows, rows of blobs stretched far and wide. Megan reached down and pulled her cell phone out of her pocket. She engaged the flashlight app and gasped. Before her, the children's souls stood motionless like frozen statues. As the light fell on each of them, their eyes popped open, but otherwise they remained suspended in animation. After spotting Suzie's, she yelled in her direction, but it did not flinch. An eerie feeling of deja-vu washed over her.

With the phone, she scanned the room. As the light hit the wall behind her, it began to crumble. The pile of dirt grew higher and higher. Gripped by a memory, she stiffened like a board. She had climbed the pile. That's how she escaped all those years ago. She shone her light back on the wall to expedite the process as she desperately tried to recall the answer. *How did she wake the children?*

As she clutched at her necklace, the nervous tick she could never abolish, clarity ensued. Between her fingers, the tiny pendant, a pea-less whistle shone like a beacon in the night. After placing it in her mouth, she blew as hard as she could. The shrill tone blasted across the cave, like a sonic boom, and the children's souls snapped awake. Screams of terror poured from their mouths as they vanished in a puff of smoke.

Megan began the arduous trek up the dirt pile. Each step sent dirt crashing back to the ground below. As she reached the surface, a long tendril reached up and wrapped itself around her ankle. She shoved the whistle back into her mouth and blew. Once again, the shrill tone rang out. The tendril pulled hard one last time before releasing her leg. Her head smashed against a rock and sent her into an unnatural slumber.

*

ONE BY ONE, THE CHILDREN STIRRED. Suzie awoke and looked around the room. Sun shone through the window and created a square of bright white on the linoleum floor. Outside, a bird trilled the same three notes over and over. The faint smell of disinfectant lingered in the air. Beside her, an empty chair, screamed the truth. She smiled at the other children with a sadness behind her eyes.

Megan, who had been found unconscious by the well in her garden, lay unresponsive across the hall. The imprint of a curb chain stretched across her palm, the necklace nowhere to be found. Dried blood crusted in the corners of her mouth. Upon further examination, Dr. Xavier discovered her right eye had turned white, an anomaly that could not be explained. A condition recorded only once before, decades before his tenure, for a patient named Annabelle.

The Plan

By Arjan Atwal

THE EARTH HAS BEEN ABUSED FOR YEARS. The conditions are too much to ignore. Forest fires, rain, snow and ice storms are now common in Los Angeles. There was a time when a snowfall would be something to marvel at. The state has become a fascist regime that has denied most science, but California is considered liberal.

Pollution and rising population have inflicted a great deal of damage. The earth is pissed. Tonight, the state is going to address the people's concerns. Science can no longer be ignored. People are ready to break out into mass hysteria. "God has a plan." That's what the state says whenever disaster strikes.

A sense of angst permeates throughout the city. People are glued to their television sets, awaiting the state of the union address, but Jake Willow has better things to do.

*

"ANOTHER TEQUILA PINEAPPLE PLEASE."

Jake lives in Los Angeles and works as an illegal car dealer. Only fully autonomous cars are allowed on the road, but there is always a market for enthusiasts who want their V8 muscle. The amount of automobile fatalities has decreased but does it *really* matter? Scientists predict that the Earth will last for less than fifty years.

Bright, colorful hologram billboards light the city streets. The Hollywood sign has all but disappeared into a thick fog. Technology dominates every facet of life. Most devices are smart and run on the state-run network. It used to be something called the Internet, but that was before Jake's time, and before the state supplanted it with their own interface. Jake uses a vintage Nokia candy-bar phone, which operates on a pirate network. Perfect for conducting some shady business.

Jake stares at his glass and contemplates his relationship with his friend, sometimes lover, Eva. Tonight is the night he is going to tell her how he feels. The barkeep is in a world of his own, glued to his cell phone. The giant screen illuminates his face.

A loud emergency alert sounds. A strange broadcast airs over all devices hooked to the network. Streams of neon pink and purple radiate from the screens.

"What is it?"

The barkeep stays silent, staring at his phone. A stream of color projects from his phone into his eyes.

Jake decides this is a good time for him to leave. He steps outside the bar. There is nothing but darkness in the once illuminated city streets. Sirens can be heard in the distance. Jake fears the worst and decides he needs to go see Eva, now. She's kind of a hippie who likes to stay off the grid, so contact won't be easy.

Jake's car won't operate. The network has never been down before. Jake can't recall an instance in his lifetime where it hasn't worked. Without an interface to operate on, the car is a lemon.

Jake decides to start his journey on foot. He walks through the concrete jungle. Chaos is all around him. Shops are being looted and destroyed. Buildings are on fire but these weren't caused by the weather. Jake decides it would be best to get a closer look. He ends up at Pete's Sporting goods. Upon closer inspection, the people weren't looting. They are killing each other. A man uses his thumbs to squeeze out another's eyeballs. Jake had never seen such savagery. What could be causing this vicious behavior? Jake feels a sharp pain in the back of his head. His vision becomes blurry. Jake drops to the ground. A short, stalky man stands over him with a large club. He wails on him.

"Stop please, you can take everything I have."

The man doesn't acknowledge anything Jake says. He thrashes Jake into a bloody pulp before getting distracted by another passerby. Jake picks himself off the floor, blood dripping from his most likely broken nose and now concave cheekbones. He searches around the cash register for some sort of weapon he can use to protect himself. He discovers an old Glock and a few boxes of ammunition. Jake also finds a children's bicycle complete with a front basket and tassels on the handlebars. It isn't ideal but it would help him get to Eva quicker. He rides on the comically small bike, his legs scrunched up almost touching his chest.

Jake reaches Eva's apartment. A man works on busting through Eva's front door. He kicks it over and over again unfazed by the pain. As Jake watches, his leg becomes mangled from kicking the reinforced door. His ankle is broken; his foot just hangs there as he keeps kicking. There is no humanity left in this man. Jake points his gun at the man. He remembers to switch the safety off and squeezes the trigger, blowing a hole straight through the man's head. Jake never fired a gun before but had seen it in movies. Jake was never a violent man but a survival instinct kicked in. The sheer shock of the situation has not fully set in yet.

"Eva!" he yells through the door.

"Jake?"

Jake can see the numerous locks turning. The door opens and Eva falls into his arms. A moment passes and Jake forgets about the carnage outside. It only lasts for about three seconds but it's an amazing three seconds. The blood from Jake's face drips on to Eva's sweater. She backs away her slender frame.

"What the fuck is going on? What happened to you?"

"We need to get out of here, there's something out there."

Eva's place is close to a car garage where illegal cars are stored. They pick a blue 2020 Camaro and load the trunk with all the gasoline they can find.

They drive through the city, witness to the carnage that has consumed LA. A group of people affected by the hysteria swarm the vehicle. Jake doesn't know what to do but he knows he can't stop. He continues to drive. The bones make a flurry of snapping sounds as he drives straight through the swarm. The windshield wipers wash away some of the blood splatter.

After being on the road for a few hours, Jake nudges Eva awake.

"Look over there."

Hundreds of men in HAZMAT suits with flamethrowers are dispersed in a neighborhood. They are burning all the houses down.

"I think we're saved." Eva says with a shred of optimism in her voice.

They spot one male adult and two children making a run for it. They are spotted by the HAZMAT men and torched on the spot. Eva's jaw drops, a sense of dread quickly replacing her optimism. The eagle crest branding of the state is proudly displayed on the HAZMAT men. A light bulb goes off in Jake's brain. The state of the union address was supposed to propose a plan for us to survive and this is it. This is the plan. Population control.

The Third Sunday in June

By Sterling Mahl

Lenny Watson sat down with both elbows resting on the Formica table and questioned whether the interrogation room felt a little small. His attorney, had he opted to retain one, would surely have insisted he focused instead on presenting a coherent story to whomever would be sent in first to get a crack at pulling a confession out of him. It was only a question of time – Lenny himself knew better than any lawyer worth two figs and a walnut – before he ended up in front of a newly-minted county judge with a nervous case of fire and brimstone ironed into his robes who would be clever enough to count up the strikes and lock him away until the end of days. Each time he came down for 'a chat' over at the precinct could very well be his last appearance in one of these rooms – and not because he had finally perfected the scheme that would carry him through his golden years. Frowning at his wrinkles in the two-way mirror, he sighed and admitted, to himself as much as to his absent attorney, there was nothing wrong with the room. But if this was to be the time he finally struck out, he wished the fanfare could have resonated a tad more boisterously than it would in this tiny concrete chamber.

The door opened. Lenny looked up and could not decide whether he was relieved or insulted it was only a local Sheriff's deputy walking in rather than a full-fledged detective called in from Topeka. Mind you, he was more than just a kid – early thirties perhaps, generous brown goatee with early sprinkles of gray, a slightly tarnished wedding ring – but, still, just a uniform. He carried a hefty file folder under his arm, filled with glossy facsimile paper. Like a long trail of stale breadcrumbs, re-surfaced every time Lenny slipped up: extortion in upstate New York, embezzlement in Palm Beach, bribery in New Orleans, and so on and on. Some of it he had done time for – six months in Holman Correctional Facility, Alabama; nine in Mule Creek State Prison, California – but, for the most part, he had managed to slip through the net of justice.

"Mister Watson," the deputy said, disguised under the fake smile of a man who would rather be starting his weekend early, and dropped the file on the table with just enough strength to emphasise how thick it actually was. "I hope you didn't have to wait too long. It can get a bit uncomfortable on them chairs."

Lenny had met this type before: late rookie, probably an army grunt recently recycled as a county cop who mistakenly thought passive aggressive intimidation was a clever way to open an interrogation. Officer Sinclair – for that is what the plastic nametag pinned above his right breast said – was likely not the finest this place had to offer but, let's face it, Lenny himself was no Al Capone either. He briefly considered not answering but that would only prompt the deputy to escalate his performance to a level neither would enjoy. "Well, it's a bit dry I find. I could use a glass of water… if you have a clean glass to spare."

Sinclair starred at him, looking unsure of his next move.

"A glass of water, if you please" Lenny insisted, and busted his go-to smile.

"Well, it's a shame all we have is Dixie cups," the cop replied, "by the water fountain in the lobby. You're welcome to help yourself… on the way out."

He looked proud of himself, Lenny reckoned. That was fine. He could handle Dixie cup-sized setbacks all day long and still make this guy wish he had signed up for one more tour in Iraq. In fact, this could well be a good sign; if the Sheriff's office actually considered this cocky, wet-behind-the-ears rookie the right man for the job, then surely they must have thought the dossier was not nearly as impressive as it was thick, and Lenny would be on his way out of state well before dusk.

"Mr. Watson," Sinclair carried on, "before we start with our official business here, I want to make sure you understand the gravity of your situation."

"And just what is our business here, deputy?" Lenny asked, trying to steer him away from whatever game plan he may have walked in with. "I came here voluntarily to help clarify any misconception local authorities" – he waved whimsically at Sinclair – "appear to have construed about my presence in this town…"

Sinclair looked like he was coming unglued. This was too easy by far. "…but I find myself shoved in the hot seat without as much as a friggin' glass of water!" he added, merely for dramatic effect. He almost blurted an accusatory 'how dare you, sir?' on top of it but caught himself when his gut protested he may be spreading the histrionics a smidge too thick already. Not to mention emptying his quiver before he knew exactly what he was facing would only make him look guilty of just about anything. Better keep some outrage for later.

Sinclair opened his mouth to reply but Lenny, the old pro, caught the hesitation, a mere half-second of self-doubt, largely imperceptible to the general population but which told in simple terms the real story unfolding in the room. "Mr. Watson, please calm down."

"I am calm."

"I just want you to fully understand that cooperating is in your best interest before–"

"–I have been trying to cooperate ever since your colleagues barged into my hotel room–"

"–I don't think 'barged' is the right term here, Mr. Watson–"

"– and I don't think you were there, deputy."

Lenny imagined his absent attorney would have requested a quick word and strongly reiterated that engaging in a pissing match with representatives of the law was ill-advised behaviour at the best of times. Not unexpectedly, he waved off the thought.

"Son, I don't think we need to dwell too much on the gravity of the situation. The way I understand it is if the situation was as *grave* as you seem to imply, they clearly would not have sent *you*."

They stared at each other for a few seconds – Sinclair desperately grasping at whatever shreds of authority remained within his reach, Lenny basking in his own smug cleverness – before someone rapped quietly on the door. The cavalry, no doubt. This could be bad – cooler heads made a nasty habit of poking fat fingers through the gaps in his stories until he was left with no choice but to take an early bow and run out the fire exit. Hopefully, this was only the second act of the good cop/bad cop routine. Sinclair, visibly annoyed, slowly rose up from his chair, turned sharply with an audibly exaggerated sigh as if to indicate the staring contest was not yet over, and opened the door just enough to hold a muted argument with the person standing on the other side.

"But they have no jurisdiction here!" Lenny heard Sinclair protest under his breath before he sighed again and walked out, only to be replaced with a breathing caricature of every con man's worst nightmare.

What an unattractive fella! Lenny thought as he recoiled and sat straighter in his chair. The various individual oddities which the man's appearance displayed would not have usually proven nearly remarkable enough to render speechless a conversationalist of Lenny's stature, but trying to process them all at once was overwhelming. He produced a thin leather wallet from the interior breast pocket of his dark blue striped suit and when he flipped it open with a quick thrust of his wrist, Lenny realised it was a badge he had never seen – or forged – before. "I am Agent Duchaine, Department of Homeland Security," the man said in a crusty tone that suggested he was past trying to impress anyone with his job title. Then, casually gesturing to a woman standing on his right and who Lenny hadn't noticed at all until then, added: "This is Agent Purnell."

She moved swiftly in front of her partner and asked: "Do you mind if I sit down, Mr. Watson?"

Lenny knew immediately these two were setting up a different kind of ball game; histrionics would get him nowhere, so he might as well play along until he figured out a couple of the basic rules. Looking up at Agent Purnell, he smiled and graciously extended his hand towards the chair Sinclair had just vacated. The way she held her hands tightly clasped together gave away the impression she had more to say than she actually would.

"I usually open these interviews by reassuring the person in front of me they are not in any kind of trouble," Agent Purnell said, "but in your case, Mr. Watson, I can't say this is true."

Lenny tried desperately to look like he'd heard it all before.

"Another way which marks this interview as peculiar," she continued, "is the fact I'm about to admit to you we are in trouble as well. So, in the spirit of expediency, I will cut straight to the heart of the matter: we require your assistance in apprehending the criminal who calls himself Charlie Balzac."

It was hard to tell whether she was waiting for him to respond or merely pausing for dramatic effect, but Lenny had to stifle a nervous laugh, nonetheless. Some would say he'd lived a crazy life, and Frig knows he'd said some outrageous things to gullible people – truth be told, the reason he was sitting right here was someone caught him *in flagrante delicto* selling plots of moon land for two grand an acre to a room full of mesmerised seniors over at Golden Oaks Villa – but this, the suggestion he could (or would, for that matter) be instrumental in bringing *the* Charlie Balzac to justice, was a big fat whopper in a class of its own. "You can't be serious, ma'am," he said.

Charlie Balzac had become a household name seven years prior when the artificial intelligence machines he'd sold to the military central commands of Columbia, Chile, Argentina, and Brazil conducted simultaneous *coup d'états* and installed him as supreme ruler of a unified south American mega-state. Since then, he'd managed to steal enough of the recipe to bake a dozen nuclear warheads – a talking point all candidates had repeated *ad nauseam* during the last presidential race – and leaders of the free world had been forced to request updates about this first-of-his-kind-super-villain at their daily intelligence briefs.

"I'm just a–"

"–I know exactly what you are, Mr. Watson." She tapped three times on the dossier Sinclair had left behind. "You have an exceptional talent for making people believe just about anything they want to hear."

"See, that's just the thing! Correct me if I'm wrong, but I'd bet good money that Charlie Balzac isn't keeping an eye out for a dark cell five miles underground like the one you people would like to lock him in. There is absolutely no friggin' way anyone will talk him into that!"

She turned to Agent Duchaine and grabbed a razor-thin file he fished out of his attaché-case. "Have you ever seen a picture of Charlie Balzac, Mr. Watson?" she asked without opening the file.

Now here's a rhetorical question, Lenny thought to himself. Balzac was so notoriously anonymous – nothing more than a name in newspaper headlines, really – late night comedians had made a habit of including him in jokes that featured the likes of Santa Claus and the Easter Bunny. "No," Lenny admitted, "but I'll bet you have a picture of him in there, don't you?"

"Indeed, I do," Agent Purnell said softly. "From what we've been able to gather, he is approximately 36 years-old, and he was educated here in the United States but left some time after high school and landed in Santiago, Chile shortly thereafter."

"That's fascinating, really, but is this supposed to mean something to me?"

"We have intelligence which suggests he received a Catholic education at a boarding school called Holy Trinity College in Connecticut."

Lenny perked up. He knew that name, somehow. *Was that the place...? No, it couldn't be.* Then Agent Purnell opened up the file and he saw that he was wrong.

"What in Frig's blessed name are you saying?" Lenny whispered, more to himself than to Agent Purnell. The picture she'd laid right under his eyes depicted what appeared to be a young version of Lenny himself, sipping from a tiny espresso cup and seated at a crowded outdoors terrace. A flight of pigeons was taking off behind him. "If this is a trick, I swear I will sue your ass all the way to–"

"– This is not a trick, Mr. Watson. This is a recent picture of Charlie Balzac taken in Buenos Aires. As I said earlier, we need your help in apprehending him before he brings us to the brink of Armageddon. And the reason you'll do it is because he's your son."

*

(THE FIRST FRIDAY)

Thank God he wasn't stuck in a dry county! With the boy back in his life, the thought of having to weigh things out while stirring two ounces of

Dr. Pepper at the bottom of his glass was enough to make Lenny swear he'd never hit the road without a flask full of Glenfiddich within arm's reach. In fact, didn't he have one of those lying around? Likely under the seat of his car, or maybe in the storage back in Chicago? Judy had picked it up from one of those engraving kiosks at the mall a few weeks after the boy was born, cast in stainless steel with his initials carved on the front, in case fatherhood proved to make him feel old – or thirsty. And it had, on both counts. Newlywed at twenty-three, the promises attached to his community college Business & Accounting diploma had yet to materialise into a steady income by the time Judy surprised him one sunny morning with the announcement. A bundle of joy, indeed! He would have preferred the bundle included a user's manual and a million dollars' worth of vouchers and coupons.

The idea for his first scam had come from seeing an ad for beachfront timeshares in the classifieds. All it involved was renting out a lovely lakeside cottage he didn't actually own and pocketing the deposit. No *real* harm there when you considered the alternatives. That would have been enough to put meat on the table *and* afford disposable diapers without robbing half a dozen local branches of the First Midwestern, but it also flicked a switch in Lenny's brain. It was not that easy money had made him grow increasingly greedy, as Judy first thought when she stumbled upon his secret career. To be sure, the extra cash was a prime factor explaining why he no longer woke up covered in a cold sweat, or exhausted from hours of nervous tossing and turning, but it was something else that kept him going back to the till. Something joyful and liberating, and which had paved his journey from sorry-ass loser to self-made man extraordinaire. He didn't particularly enjoy taking other people's money, as he had tried to explain to Judy so many times. The rush came from closing the deal and *feeling* like a million bucks! One would be crazy to think the crushing disappointment she felt as a result had had any link to the brain cancer that took her away seven months later, but the thought, nevertheless, haunted him every time he felt the rush rising through his gut.

Life on the road had taken its toll on both of them, the boy especially. Judy's passing had created a void Lenny felt he could only fill by convincing more and more gullible folks to separate from money they did not deserve to keep. His ongoing success had imposed a nomadic lifestyle of cheap roadside motels during 'working season' rotating with 3-star Caribbean resorts for the rest of the year. *Not too bad for a free lunch*, had quickly become one of Lenny's favourite expressions. But every passing Labour Day brought a stark reminder the boy needed an education, lest he'd be forced to buy into the family business. Frig knows Judy would have risen from the dead just to make sure he'd never hear the end of it. So he had taken the path a less pragmatic man would have balked at and enrolled his son at a boarding school one of his wealthier clients/victims had once recommended in New England. He'd settled tuition up front for the year and simply walked away, confident the faculty would eventually help find the boy a loving home that would keep him away from the life of a criminal.

Go figure.

He lifted his eyes from the empty glass and scanned the reflection in the mirror behind the bar for anyone who may be following him. He'd accepted Agent Purnell's offer of amnesty for his past misbehaviour in exchange for delivering Charlie – his son, the criminal mastermind – over to the proper authorities, but that didn't mean they necessarily trusted him, or he them. A couple was sitting coyly in the corner, staring at their drinks more than each other. They both looked a bit drunk, so he dismissed them as a possible tail but filed them in the back of his mind anyway in case they re-surfaced later.

So this is it! he thought, slouching back in his seat. He'd expected there would be a reckoning of some sort after three decades of intense shenanigans, but this final showdown was pretty damn far from the version he'd made up in his mind. Instead of rotting away behind bars, he was told to roll up his sleeves and clean up the mess he'd left behind. Of course, he could make the argument that said mess didn't rest entirely at his feet – after all, he'd abandoned the boy at 7 years old – but this was also an opportunity to amend for the pain he had caused poor Judy. If there were any alternatives, he'd find them along the way; he'd made a career out of keeping back doors open.

So… time to lay down options and formulate a plan: the easiest – and admittedly smartest – thing he could do was hitch a quiet ride back to Chicago, pick up the cash he'd stashed away in storage and disappear into the mist. But they would expect that, now, wouldn't they? He glanced up in the mirror; the couple was still there, quietly sipping on their dry martinis and not looking his way.

Or he could strike in the exact opposite direction: team-up with Charlie and slowly expand the boy's crime syndicate to the four corners of the globe. Father and son shaping the underworld, just like it was meant to be. Except that it wasn't. Lenny was a charming hustler and dedicated con artist, not a *Mafioso*. And how would that go exactly? *Hello, son! Sorry I forgot to pick you up from school, so let me make it up and teach you how to be a proper crook! I promise you'll like it…* During his thirty-five years in the field, Lenny had floated his fair share of laughable lines but, even in the early days, few had sunk to this sad brand of lameness.

The right thing to do, he knew Judy was yelling at him from Above, was to try and steer the boy back onto the path he should have laid out for him in the first place. Convincing him to stop terrorising the world would be a suitable first step. *And maybe Fatherhood Award next year?*

He got up and winked clumsily at the woman in the corner on his way out. Giving away the advantage over a pair of presumptive spooks was probably a mistake, but he shrugged it off on account of the whiskey. And now that the jig was up, he thought, they might as well make themselves useful. He backtracked to their table and asked where in town he could buy a flask. He should get one for the boy, with the initials CTW – Charles Tobias Watson – carved on the front, in case they somehow managed to get out of this mess both unscathed.

*

(THE THIRD SATURDAY)

"You think this is Disneyworld?" The short man, who sported a thin handlebar moustache and had introduced himself as Octavio Flores, spoke with a heavy Brazilian Portuguese accent. "You think you can just show up at the door and get five minutes with Mickey Mouse?"

Does that make you Donald Duck, then, you irritating little prick? Lenny thought to himself. His contact in NYC had warned him Flores was well-known in 'the business' to compensate for his diminutive height by projecting an amplified aura of overall bad-assery – which did not, let's be clear, render him any less vicious than he appeared! But right now, this act smelled more like a travelling circus than a well-honed security detail. After landing in Rio de Janeiro, Lenny had been directed to the lobby of the *Hotel Atlantico*, where a non-descript henchman dropped off a copy of today's *Correi o Braziliense* on the coffee table in front of him. Buried deep in the sports section was a ferry ticket that granted him passage across the bay from *Praça de Novembro*. Two more henchmen, wearing impeccable black suits and identical pairs of Ray-Bans, had been waiting on the other side next to a black minivan with curtained windows. They held a small laminated sign indicating they were picking up a 'Mr. Brown' (aka Leonard Watson) of the United Fruit Company; from there they drove around for close to a half-hour in more zigzags and U-turns than Lenny would ever care for. They finally let him out next to a folding table and two chairs – one of which occupied by Flores – set-up right in the middle of what appeared to be a dilapidated warehouse.

"I assure you, I don't pose any threat to Mr. Balzac," Lenny tried to say as casually as he could.

"Shut the fuck up, old man! I decide who's a threat, not you, not these two *caballeros*, not even the Boss! Me!" He pointed at his own chest with dictatorial rigidity before turning the gesture towards Lenny. "Now you tell me why you're here."

"There's no need–"

"– Why are you here, Mr. Watson?" Flores wagged a stern finger so close to Lenny's nose he feared for a split second the prosthetic DHS staffers had applied to his face might fall off. Although he was using his real name, he didn't want Charlie's staff to spot the resemblance. Clearly, Flores' line of questioning suggested the tactic was working. "Think carefully about your answer; take a minute if you have to, because the next thing you say better not be a waste of my time."

Who's wasting whose time, now? Lenny began to wonder. Would it expedite the screening process to prematurely reveal himself as Charlie's father? How many imposters – distant cousins, childhood best friends – seeking a quick word with his master caused Flores to lose his shit every week? Lenny had talked his way into shadier places before, which, a slight bit of perspective would have helped him realise, was exactly the problem he now faced. This was no squalid-fly-by-night-smutty-hole-in-the-wall casino or cabaret-late-night-peep-show he was trying to get his right foot in. From what Agent Purnell had told him, Charlie's compound was a presidential palace by all agreed upon standards. It begged the question: what could a criminal mastermind possibly require which he hadn't already dispatched a lackey to fetch?

"It is my understanding Mr. Balzac has been experiencing mood swings lately…" Lenny ventured.

Agent Purnell had actually used the word *depressed*. Intelligence obtained from a source she claimed was reliable had described several behavioural episodes which the fancy operational psychologists at the CIA had flagged as cause for serious concern. *A depressed megalomaniac with access to nuclear weapons makes me nervous,* she had told him in confidence. *I have witnessed the damage a common man with nothing left to lose can inflict should he get his hands on a semi-automatic weapon; the one with a handful of thermonuclear bombs strapped to Intercontinental Ballistic Missiles, although obviously in a different league altogether, is just as concerning and must be subjected to all available stabilising strategies.* In other words, Lenny needed to pick up his boy from the frat house before he locked the door from the inside and set the place on fire.

Flores leaned back in his chair and crossed his legs. "You seem to believe you know more than you do, Mr. Watson. I don't know where you got this information, but I am pretty certain you gave your money away to a fabricator."

"Listen, I'm not offering to be his shrink. I'm sure you guys can get all the expertise you need whenever you need it, that's not why I'm here at all."

Flores slowly stood up with the palms of his hands lying flat on the table. "Then it appears, Mr. Watson, we have circled back to where we started, haven't we?"

"He needs me! I can't go into details right now, but you have to believe me."

"I don't have to do anything!" Flores erupted. "What I *should* do is kill you *right here* and leave your stinking corpse for the rats to throw a feast! The reason I will not is out of respect for your fat friend in New York who vouched for you. You say the Boss needs you? I did my research, Mr. Watson. You know what I found out? Let's see: Leonard Watson, widowed 30 years, former accountant turned con artist, clever but never rose beyond the status of amateur. Should I continue?"

Go on, you son of a bitch, Lenny encouraged him mentally. *It's not my friggin' legacy you should be worried about.*

"Specialised in defrauding seniors..." Flores made a face. "I am impressed. Pyramid schemes, once-in-a-lifetime investment opportunities, razzle-dazzle, glitter and strobe lights presentations on the get-rich-quick seminar circuit... Does it ring a bell, Mr. Watson? Because if it does, then I see absolutely nothing you have to offer that my boss needs. So I am going to give you one last chance to tell me why you are here before I kick your skinny ass back to Miami. Is that clear?"

Lenny flapped his jacket open so the inside pocket was exposed to Flores as well as the two henchmen and retrieved a photograph he placed face down on the table. "It's like I said, I know he's depressed and I'm not going to debate that with you," he said with far more belligerence than he would have considered advisable a minute prior. "You can decide to let me help you, or you can decide we all go to hell. And you'll notice I say 'we' because wherever it is this ship of the damned is going, all of us bastards are stuck on board with no ports-of-call in sight. I'm not asking you to trust me – Frig knows I wouldn't trust *you* with my lucky two-dollar bill – all I'm asking is you think for a minute what you're going to tell Carla…"

Flores' attention suddenly perked up a notch when he heard the name, as if he'd just been poked in the back of the neck with a shiv.

"…when the two of you find each other, up there in Heaven, and she asks why you let your boss blow us all up to smithereens."

If it appears you may not be able to get past Flores, Agent Purnell had mentioned while briefing Lenny on the rogues' gallery they had identified as Charlie's entourage, *the daughter is the card you'll want to play. Her name is Carla, she is 9 years old. Interestingly, she is enrolled at Holy Trinity College, Balzac's alma mater. We believe Balzac himself insisted she be sent over there as an insurance policy in case his Head of Security developed unhealthy ambitions.*

Flores flipped the picture and saw his daughter smiling merrily while posing in very close quarters with a man who looked like a freakish version of Balzac suddenly aged 25 years.

"What the fuck is this, old man?" he asked with a purposeful and frightening tremor in his voice that made Lenny immensely grateful the table lay between them.

"I'm sorry it must come to this, Mr. Flores. I also have a child. For all your fancy friends out there checking me out, I'll bet you didn't know that, did you?"

"What the fuck have you done to her?"

"Not a thing. She's perfectly safe. She's probably doing... divine math or whatever they do in Catholic school, not important. You're a smart man, Mr. Flores, and, I have no doubt, a better father than I am. Take me to see Balzac. I swear to you I have nothing but good intentions. You take me to him, and nothing happens to your little girl. It's that simple."

*

THEY MOVED FAST ONCE FLORES MADE UP HIS MIND AND HEADED straight for the freight elevator at the back of the warehouse. After a minute, the doors opened deep underground – so deep in fact, Lenny doubted this part of the building featured on the original blueprint – upon a small, but high-ceilinged space separated in half by a large trench. A few seconds later, an opaque light shone from one of the sides through a tunnel opening and he noticed rail tracks in the middle of the trench; these muddafriggers must have built a secret underground railway to move as they pleased around the city. A driverless single train car stopped in front of them. Flores stepped in and gestured for Lenny to climb aboard. The two henchmen in the striped suits stayed behind, likely required to attend additional goon duties elsewhere.

Lenny had his choice of a dozen seats as the train began to move forward. Flores excused himself and sat instead at a computer terminal located at the back end.

"How many of these do you have roaming around the city?" Lenny asked.

Flores took a few seconds to respond. He seemed preoccupied with the data stream that was scrolling up the screen in front of him. "You have already made a mistake by threatening my daughter. It would be another one to presume my decision to let you in the door means we are now friends."

This new business of holding children hostage was one Lenny hoped he could never get used to. Although he didn't believe the girl was in any real danger – at least not from him – he'd felt physically nauseated lying to Carla about being an old friend of her mother and, knowing perfectly what it was to be used for, valiantly fought the urge to hurl back his breakfast while Sister Mary Frances had snapped a couple shots of them smiling with her old Polaroid. If things were to go sideways in the next couple of days, he'd have to pull a few strings and move the girl out of Duchaine and Purnell's reach before Uncle Sam decided he'd seen enough of this circus.

"I'm really not the man you think I am," Lenny confessed.

"So who the fuck are you, then?" Flores asked without much of a curious vibe in his voice. He was still distantly mesmerised by the plasma screen.

I'm not you, for starters, Lenny thought but knew better than spitting it out loud.

"Well, clearly you understand what it's like to have a child–"

Flores turned around sharply, with fiery death screaming in his eyes.

"Let me finish, please." Lenny gathered his thoughts for a moment. "The moment your child is born... everything you do is part of a grand master plan, right, to try and steer them on a path to have a better life than you did. You see the world in a different light, even from the day before, and every choice you make from then on is dedicated to helping your child avoid making the mistakes you made."

Lenny had spent thirty years chatting up strangers on just about anything from cold water stream fly fishing to civil war battlefield miniature replicas. On very few occasions had he felt the need to open up a small window into his own soul in order to make a connection and close the deal. Today should have been no different; he didn't need Flores lavishly wined and dined to get his hands on the key to the vault. Agent Purnell had handed him the one card that mattered, and he'd already played it. Why did he feel he had to explain himself to this grunt who, more likely than not, wouldn't hesitate a second to lock up the doors of a burning school if he thought it would help him score a couple brownie points with the Boss?

"And depending on how... conceited? Yes, I guess you can say that, how conceited you are," he continued, "This can go one of two ways. You can encourage and nurture them to become the best person they can be or... you can try and shape them into a better version of yourself." He looked up at Flores. "And if you succeed – in the second case, I mean, 'cause if it's the first case then you've pretty much aced it as a parent–"

"–Yes, yes, get on with it!"

"But if you succeed at making them a better version of yourself, then you'd better be ready to... to do whatever's necessary to right the wrong you've created."

Flores stared at him silently for a few seconds, deconstructing his face and replacing the separate pieces with younger ones.

"Are you saying...?"

The lights inside the train went suddenly dark and the car itself was noticeably slowing down. Flores got immediately up on his feet and scanned the tunnel ahead as well as behind them.

"Is there a problem?" Lenny asked. "Why have we stopped?"

Was this part of the whole theatrics as well, he wondered. The drop at the hotel, the ferry across the bay, the drive in the blacked-out van, did they really need one more test to... to do what exactly?

"Flores, what's happening?"

"I am not certain. Be quiet!"

He kicked a metal box bolted to the floor underneath the computer console and the backup emergency lights crackled to life. Lenny noticed Flores was holding a black pistol in his hand and had tucked another one in the front of his trousers.

"Do I need one of those?" he asked sheepishly.

"I do not recall any mention of your ability to handle a firearm," Flores replied, still pacing back and forth between the two extremities of the car. He looked back at Lenny with quizzical eyes. "Can you handle it?"

"It can't be that hard."

"Can I trust you?"

"I won't shoot you in the back, if that's what you're asking."

Flores handed him the pistol he held in his hand and immediately retrieved the other one at his waist. "It is ready to fire, just pull the trigger."

"What's going on here, for Frig's snakes?"

"Do not worry. A team of my men will be here to pick us up in five minutes. We just need to–"

The back window exploded in a thousand shards of glass. Flores was firing. The front window shattered almost simultaneously. Lenny aimed as best he could – unsure where and at what – with shaking hands and pulled the trigger but his pistol was jammed. Flores was replacing his magazine. Lenny pulled the trigger again, still jammed. *What the frig?* Large shadowy forms were crawling in through the windows, overwhelming Flores while he tried to recharge again. The world went completely dark around Lenny – a cloth sack over his head, he realised – as too many hands for him to slip away from grabbed his limbs from all directions and carried him off the floor. He felt a needle prick through the skin at the base of his neck and screamed Flores' name in terror. There was no response other than undecipherable whispers amongst his assailants as they handed his body through a broken window to another group of hands waiting outside. His mind became unbearably heavy and faded with cold panic into a black hole of slumber.

*

LENNY JERKED HIS HEAD BACKWARDS AS HE WAS SUDDENLY ROUSED up from the darkness. Breathing heavily, he tried to bring his hands to his face but could not move them. He looked down and saw long strands of – what was that, duct tape? – wrapped around his limbs and torso, effectively tying him up to a metal folding chair. Renewed fright squirmed up quickly from his guts to his throat, leaving an instant trail of cold sweat on his chest and neck while triggering the memory of his last few conscious moments.

"Werizfloressss?" he wondered incoherently, still groggy and more than a little disoriented, when a brisk scan of his surroundings failed to locate him.

Instead he noticed a woman standing next to a set of rickety floor cupboards, putting away a glass vial and syringe in a small silver case. She turned to look at him, the lower half of her face covered under a black bandanna to match her shoulder-length curly hair. Taken aback, he considered in rapid succession the various scenarios which could explain where the frig he was; none of them ended well for him. The woman walked quietly towards him and examined his neck before removing her rubber gloves.

"Woowariooo?" Lenny asked, still incapable of intelligible speech.

She retrieved a pen light from her pocket and shone the blinding beam into each of his eyes. He recoiled as much from fright as from pain and almost sent the chair barreling backwards.

"Cuidado!" the woman said with a touch of gentle care in her voice. "Eu não vou te machucar."

Lenny had seen enough plastic cones left on wet floors by custodial staff to recognise she was telling him to be careful, which he reckoned must be a good sign. A psychotic murderer would have more likely taken sadistic pleasure in fueling his terror instead.

"Idunnowayoreshaying..." he managed to whisper, unable to decipher what she had said after that.

She placed the palms of her hands on his cheeks and said, "Pare de tentar falar, eu volto já," while slowly nodding her head up and down. Then she spun around and headed towards the door but stopped and looked at him, nodding again, before walking out of the room.

No! Don't you friggin' leave! Lenny yelled at her in his head. He looked around him: the room was approximately ten by twelve feet, with fluorescent neon tubes attached to the low ceiling. There were no windows.

The woman walked back in almost immediately, followed by an older man frowning beneath a thick, grey beard that somehow suggested he was in charge of this outlet. Lenny could tell he was in for a bumpy ride.

"Onde está o Dr. Sereno?" the man bearded asked without any

introduction.

They're speaking Portuguese, Lenny figured. He took a deep breath and tried to concentrate on enunciating one simple word at a time.

"I... don't... understand." It came out still a bit garbled but much clearer than the muddled gibberish he'd spewed out since waking up.

"You speak English?" the woman asked with a heavy accent, approaching him again.

Lenny nodded with widening eyes and relief washing over his face. "Where... are we? Who are... you?"

The bearded man repeated his initial question, apparently oblivious to Lenny's own.

"We will not hurt you," the woman reassured him by placing a hand on his shoulder. "We only want to ask some questions."

"I don't know anything! This is crazy!" Lenny insisted. His speech was mostly back to its regular form, though a close friend would have suspected he was nursing a mild hangover.

The woman patted his shoulder a couple times and whispered to him everything would be over soon if he answered the questions, then took a step back and looked at the bearded man as if to plead with him to be gentle.

"Onde está o Dr. Sereno?" the man asked again.

Lenny looked at the woman.

"He is asking about Dr. Sereno," she translated. "Do you know where he is?"

"No. Who is that?"

The bearded man blurted another question.

"Is the mind upload experiment completed?" the woman translated again.

Lenny took a moment to process the question. Did she say *mind upload*? *What the frig*? He felt trapped in the punch line of a sick joke these twisted folks probably liked to play on their kidnap victims, just waiting for the metal helmet and copper wire coming out of it.

"I don't know what he's talking about," he said evenly, trying to drive a subtle wedge between the two of them while at the same time solidifying his grip on the lifeline she appeared ready to throw at him. "I'm Leonard Watson, from Chicago. This is crazy! You have to let me go!"

She translated back to Portuguese for the benefit of the bearded man, who appeared to grow increasingly annoyed.

"I don't know anything about a mind upload… Who are you people?" Lenny pleaded.

The bearded man walked right up to him and stared into his eyes. "Você é um mentiroso imundo!" he said like he was stating an obvious fact. "Qual é o seu papel na organizão?"

Lenny tried to look around him and re-connect with his fleeting lifeline, standing a few paces on the left behind the bearded man.

"He said you are a liar. He wants to know your role in the organisation."

His role is in the organisation? Did she mean Charlie's outfit? Of course, that must be why they took him from the train! *Frig!* This psycho thought he was part of Charlie's gang of thugs and… and what? His son was a criminal mastermind, what did this mind upload dumbfuckery have to do with anything?

"I'm not part of the organisation. You mean Balzac's, right? I've got nothing to do with them. I'm just a lonely American taking in the sights."

"Why were you on that train?" the woman asked, this time of her own volition.

Lenny checked out all the mental stops on his usual bullshit circuit but quickly realised he didn't have any room to dance around that question.

"I'm not with them, I swear. Whatever he's done to you... I'm sorry... I don't know what else to say."

"The train," she insisted. "We need to know what happened to Dr. Sereno, it is important."

"I don't know any Dr. Sereno, I swear! You got the wrong guy. I'm nobody. If you're after intel, it's Flores you want to squeeze."

The name, *Flores*, spoken out loud seemed to suddenly revive the bearded man's hunting instincts. He grabbed Lenny's chin with a surprisingly strong grip and lifted it upwards as if to resume the staring contest.

"Por que você estava com Flores?"

Lenny didn't have to wait for the translation. "That son of a bitch is a psycho!" he shouted back at the bearded man. "I was using him to... I need to get to Balzac... before..."

"Before what?" the woman asked.

Before he kills us all, Lenny wanted to yell. *Before my son kills us all on a whim!*

"I'm done talking to you," he said instead. "I don't know who the frig you are and I don't know what the frig you want... but I know I'm done talking to you!"

He closed his eyes as if to let the bearded man know the shop had gone out of business for good. He supposed they might try to torture out of him whatever information they thought he had – and he'd make something up when that time came, everybody splinters one way or another under torture – but he was done for now.

"Você vai me dizer o que eu quero saber!" the bearded man reiterated as he let go of Lenny's chin and started unbuttoning his own shirt.

"Lucas, não!" the woman shouted, closing the short gap in one long stride and grabbing his right arm with both her hands. "Ele não sabe de nada!"

He sent her flying back against the wall as if she weighed no more than a child and dealt with the remaining buttons, revealing a thick golden plate that covered approximately ten square inches in the center of his torso. It slowly opened up under the light pressure of his five fingertips onto what must have been some kind of built-in biometrics scanner. *What in the Lord's friggin' name are you?* Lenny thought as the bearded man reached deep into his chest cavity and uncoiled a round black wire the size of his pinkie with three sharp silver claws at the tip that seemed to close and retract of their own volition.

"Don't come near me, you freak!" Lenny yelled in anguish, frantically trying to free his limbs from their duct tape bonds. He glanced furtively at the woman lying on the floor against the wall to his left; she was conscious but visibly frightened, unable to gather the strength for another rescue attempt. The bearded man, now behind him, grabbed the top of Lenny's head with the same unyielding grip he had used to maintain his chin in place. "Get your hands off me! I swear you'll–"

The three silver claws suddenly dug into the back of his neck and burrowed up to the spot where his spine intersected with his skull, leaving him to gasp as his face froze in quiet agony. He then felt a cold metallic prong spring out between the claws and slowly insert itself into whatever neural component lay past the soft tissue. Gears started to whirr and shuffle behind him and he felt a powerful jolt surge through his brain, neither pleasant nor painful, more like he'd instantly been force-fed a boatload of espresso beans. The bearded man relaxed his grip but nonetheless managed to maintain Lenny's entire body firmly in place.

Strangely, his next thought was of Agent Purnell, of a slightly scrambled and fading black and white picture of her disembodied head weaving in 3D right in front of his eyes, and he tried to recall whether this had been part of the pre-deployment briefing. She'd covered Charlie's mental state in more details than he had thought necessary; she'd covered Octavio Flores, Charlie's diminutive Head of Security, and his one weakness, tucked away in Connecticut for safe-keeping; she'd covered DHS' asset within Charlie's entourage, anonymous but deemed reliable, ready to make contact once Lenny got in and become his *de facto* handler to help him complete the mission; she'd covered... *Flores was sitting at the computer terminal while... Charlie was five years old, putting the finishing touches to a paint-by-number tableau roaming dinosaurs off the edge of a coffee table... Agent Duchaine was pointing at various firearms laid on a table and explaining the difference between semi and fully automatic... Charlie was standing up on a wooden stool as the tailor measured his waist for the school uniform... Sister Mary Frances was rummaging through a dusty cupboard muttering 'I know it's in here somewhere...'*

What the frig is happening? Lenny screamed inside his mind. *Make this insanity stop!*

His memories near and distant kept merging in and out of each other in a crazy maelstrom inside his mind. Was the bearded man doing this... searching? Scanning? Copying the content of his hippocampus as he would a hard drive about to be discarded?

Agent Purnell was holding up a mirror to his face after they first tried the prosthetics... Judy was pouring coffee in a brand-new cup that said 'World's Best Dad...'

A deafening sound rocked the small room, not quite an explosion but rather as if a wrecking ball had just slammed into the front of the building. Seconds later a ruckus of screams and gun shots erupted just outside the door.

Mrs. Riley was leading him to a podium set-up in front of a roomful of codgers waiting to hear his sales pitch at the Golden Oaks Residence for assisted living...

The door splintered wide open as a man clad in black military gear and holding a machine gun rushed in. He took a split second to assess the situation and fired four bullets that whizzed inches away from Lenny's head. The bearded man grunted and whimpered behind him as he took the hits and stumbled to the floor. The wire remained hooked up to Lenny's neck, but he no longer felt the unstoppable drain of his memories. Another jolt of electrical current surged up, filling Lenny's brain with an exploding fireball of random streams of knowledge. There was no coherence to any of it, but a handful of flashbacks emerged out of the confusion and clung to his consciousness long enough that he would remember them after he passed out.

*

(THE THIRD SUNDAY)

Lenny woke up in bed in a room he did not recognise, having dreamt of a strange world in which his estranged adult son, a philosopher-king turned dictator of South America, planned to conquer the world using a vanguard of AI-enhanced supercomputers led by a sentient machine assembled to house the digitised mind of a human being. He wondered whether a couple of oysters from the seafood platter – compliments of

Gino's the night before he left New York – had skipped past their best before date and triggered this lunatic piece of reverie. Or maybe it was the whiskey? Frig, what if he couldn't handle his Glenfiddich the way he used to? Well, that was tomorrow's problem.

Meanwhile, there remained the trivial matter of finding out where he'd actually spent the night. Let's see, he was waking up alone but on the far side of a queen size bed. Had he...? Well, he vaguely recalled a woman... a beautiful Latina with shoulder-length black curly hair whose name was on the tip of his tongue. He giggled at the thought, wondering what else he may have tasted with the tip of his tongue. Taking a moment to recall sweet memories of times long gone, he nonetheless pushed away his inner schoolboy as far back as he could and, almost instantly, found the name he was looking for: Adriana Cardoso, the sexy nurse he'd met over at... at... Holy Frig, how much had he had to drink? The fleeting image of a drab backroom in a commercial building kept poking at the back of his mind but that couldn't be right. Why would they...

At that exact moment, her life flashed before his eyes: vivid images, intricate details, closely-held secrets... not the mere memories of a flirtatious conversation over drinks but rather the clear and unshakable conviction he knew her.

She was 43 years old and had never married – plenty of romantic suitors had come and gone since her nursing school days but none had stuck around long enough to compete with the platonic love she reserved for Dr. Sereno...

Why did that name sound so familiar?

... she believed her four nieces and nephews shared enough of her genetic material to spoil them as if they were her own... 15 years ago she'd been recruited by Dr. Felipe Sereno... (known in opposition circles as the Fallen Creator)... along with a handful of young talented graduates to join his research team at the faculdade de Ciências Médicas and help build perfect artificial limbs to assist

amputees... caught the eye of Lucas Montes, the last of the suitors, between two rounds of patient consultations and broke his heart (almost literally) by sending him tumbling down a flight of stairs after he tried to steal a kiss she would rather not part with...

This man, Lucas Montes, Lenny knew him, inexplicably, as well as he knew himself, could feel the dense richness of the man's thick, grey beard between his own hands.

Born in Rocinha during the early years of the military government... brought himself up from severe poverty... acclaimed as a promising young medical prodigy before breaking his spine in an unfortunate lovers' quarrel ... spent half a year rotting away in the forgotten wing of a state hospital until private money had diverted Dr. Sereno's humanitarian efforts towards integrating mind and mechanical means within the human body... after he'd rebuilt him...

Wait here a goddamn minute, now! Was that...? Yes, he recalled now... he'd been out last night... but not drinking or flirting with a sexy nurse. He'd been... Frig! Where had he been? Tiny pieces of the puzzle were dancing before his eyes, shifting, shuffling, slowly falling back into place to reveal the... the muddafriggin' cyborg who had probed his brain! More instant knowledge was crystallizing into deep and vivid memories, but Lenny refused to pay them any attention. He needed to head straight out of wherever this place was before an army of the mechanical dead dragged him feet first onto an operating table and harvested whatever replacement organs they ought to need!

He jumped out of bed and found a set of clothes – not his but they would do just fine – laid out on a comfy chair by the window. He peeked outside while dressing and spotted a vast foliated garden surrounded on all sides by low rise office buildings. Judging by the light, it likely was mid-day but he didn't see anyone walking or sitting outside, only birds gliding down from the tall trees to a ship-shaped pond and back up again. The door opened behind him before he had time to slip on the sandals and a well-groomed young man wearing a shirt and tie matching his short red hair walked in with a clipboard in hand.

"Mr. Watson, I'm glad to see you up and running. It seems the wardrobe is a match," he said with a genuine smile extending across his face. "Excellent!"

This one looked human from one end to another... but so had the other one before he took off his shirt.

"Would you be so kind and tell me where I am?" Lenny asked with a dash of apprehension.

"Well of course, my apologies! You were not at your best when Mr. Flores brought you back and I guess you might be a little... confused. My name is Luis Barbosa – at your service – I am the personal assistant to Mr. Balzac and this is Mr. Balzac's residential compound; the guest wing, to be more precise."

This was Charlie's place, right. He'd almost forgotten the main reason – the only reason, in fact – he'd come down here to Brazil, sent on a special mission to track down his son and serve him on a silver platter to the good 'ole boys of the USDHS.

"Yes, things are a bit... thank you!" Lenny rubbed his left temple and only then seemed to notice the triple sheet of gauze that was taped to the back of his neck. He purposely didn't react. "Where can I find my – Mr. Balzac, my good man?"

Luis tightened his lips and appeared for a second like he was questioning whether to open them again. "I have never read 'Love in the Time of Cholera' but it is on my short list for the summer holiday," he said in a stiff, unnatural delivery.

Our asset within Balzac's organisation will contact you after you arrive and identify themselves to you with a recognition phrase, Agent Purnell had mentioned during the tradecraft training sessions. *It will be critical to the success of your mission to memorise it as well as your own recognition phrase which you will provide in return.*

"I don't have much time to read these days, but I'll watch the movie adaptation," Lenny replied. Well, well, well. There stood the snitch that'd started this wild goose chase: a late-twenty-something rules stickler with a dented clipboard – a surprising contradiction which indubitably harboured a story waiting to be told – who sold his employer to the world's *gendarmerie* for reasons Lenny fully intended to find out before this was all over. At least half a dozen additional questions needed immediate answers, but he wasn't sure where to start.

"Shall we walk outside for a few minutes?" Luis proposed. "The garden is very pleasant at this time of day."

Lenny took the hint and so they strolled out of the mansion, making small talk along the way for the benefit of the guards posted at a couple checkpoints. About halfway around the pond, Lenny figured they were well out of earshot. "Ok, genius, what's the big plan?" he asked at once.

"How should I know?" Luis replied. "I'm just the messenger. You are the one who needs to–"

"– You think I can–"

"– You are his father! Are you not?"

Lenny didn't know how to answer that.

"You *are* his father, yes?" Luis asked again.

"I was, but that was a really long time ago. They made this whole thing sound like a good idea but, really... I don't know why I came here."

"This is what he wants, to find you. He wants you back in his life."

"He said that?"

"Of course, he did. Why else would I tell the DHS to find you?"

Why else indeed, my boy? He could've recited here and now the two dozen reasons – some better than others, admittedly – he'd scribbled on both sides of his in-flight napkin detailing why he didn't want to do this anymore but none stood up to what Luis had just so casually stated.

"Does he know I'm here?" Lenny asked.

"No. In fact, he has barely come out of his study these past ten days or so."

"Is he still depressed?"

"That is hard to say. He looked to be in a depressive state when I sent my last report and then Dr. Sereno died–"

"—Sereno is dead? When? How? The cyborg guy... Montes, he asked about him!"

"Yes, I guess they would – wait, did you say Montes? How do you know his name?"

Lenny had to think about this for a moment, sorting out every detail Agent Purnell had briefed him on to one side, and whatever he'd picked up on the way to the other. Was it the nurse who'd said his name?

"I don't know," he realised. "I woke up twenty minutes ago with his whole life story crammed into my brain. Must have been... he had some kind of wire coming out of his belly – I know that sounds crazy but I swear that's how it went – and it hooked up in the back of my neck. He was rummaging through my memories... I think he was looking for information on Charlie."

"Yes, Mr. Flores mentioned you were hooked up to Montes when they retrieved you–"

"—Flores! How did he find me? Why? He doesn't know who I am—"

"He said something about you having to call back home. I am not sure what he meant."

Good to know Flores wasn't ready yet to call his bluff about Carla.

"Ok, let's take a step back, shall we? How did Dr. Sereno die?"

"He had a heart attack about ten days ago, just before Mr. Balzac secluded himself."

"Were they close, he and Charlie?"

"Yes, he was the closest thing Mr. Balzac had to—"

Luis caught himself and looked mortified.

"It's ok, you can say it," Lenny agreed. "I dropped the ball and tiptoeing around it won't change a thing."

"They disagreed on many things. Even after he left his research team and joined Mr. Balzac, Dr. Sereno kept a soft spot for the cyborg project."

"What do you mean?"

"He believed humanity was flawed and required a bit of an upgrade, but he also believed it needed to remain... human. Hence the cyborg project, despite all its technical grafts and mechanical enhancements. Unfortunately, he was ahead of his time and funding dried up, continuing in that direction was a dead end."

"I think Lucas Montes would have disagreed..."

"You're right but that came much later in this story. Ten years ago, Mr. Balzac had the money Dr. Sereno needed to make things happen, even if their visions clashed. So, he came on board anyway and thought he would be able to change Mr. Balzac's mind over time."

"What is Charlie's vision?" Lenny asked.

Luis exhaled and took a long, hard look around the garden. "Let's not dwell on that. It is time for you to go meet your son."

*

LENNY HAD OFTEN IMAGINED WHAT HE WOULD TELL CHARLIE IF someday he turned with his family for a surprise reunion. In the dream scenario, Charlie had married a lobsterman's daughter from Maine, smart as hell, with a PhD in Comparative Literature or some other discipline common folks usually think anybody can do until they try it themselves and fall flat on their padded ass. Their two little girls, five-year-old twins called Ashley and Sarah, had learned only that morning they had another gramps they'd never met, and were just dying to both sit on his lap for story time. He'd start with 'Goldilocks and the Three Bears' and make his way through a handful of tales from Brothers Grimm – only appropriate ones, of course – and finish with 'Hansel and Gretel', in honour of his son finding his way home after being abandoned by a father who'd been in way over his head. He would tell Charlie... see, that's the part he'd never really figured out. And now, instead of Charlie and his flock showing up giggling and smiling at his imaginary brownstone outside Chicago, it was him knocking at the door – quite literally – of Charlie's study, wondering how he was supposed to save the world from this madman.

"I don't think he's going to open the door," Lenny said to Luis after a minute.

"Well, let's hope I will not regret this," Luis shot back as he placed his right palm flat against the wall, which activated a digital keypad. "I have an emergency code to override the lock. So does Flores." He worked his fingers against the keypad and put his hand on the handle, which only then triggered an audible click. "Two-step release mechanism," Luis explained. "Same set of fingerprints or no luck."

That's my boy, Lenny thought.

Luis encouraged him with a soft pat on the shoulder. "Don't screw it up, or I'll never hear the end of it."

Lenny shot him what he considered his best reassuring smile, then grabbed the handle with a sweaty hand and pushed the door open. His eyes immediately found a silhouette – his son, Charlie – standing behind a beautifully hand-crafted partners' desk with his back to the door while staring outside a massive bay window at the far end of the room.

"Thank you, Luis. I don't need anything right now. You'll be the first to know when I do."

He turned around to look towards the front of the room and appeared startled to find anyone other than Luis standing in the doorway. "Who let you…" he started asking but got lost mid-sentence as sparks of recognition, then anger, ignited deep inside his eyes. "Dear God… it's you, isn't it?"

Lenny's heart sank to his knees as he suddenly understood how much he had missed. Birthdays, pimples, heartbreaks, benders, graduation. "Hello… Charlie. How have you been, son?"

"This is a sobering development." Charlie walked slowly around the desk and opened a panel in the wall that revealed an elegant wet bar. "You still drink Glenfiddich?" he asked.

"How do you–"

"–I have an incredibly good memory." He poured a single drink in a crystal tumbler, which he offered to Lenny, and gestured towards a couple of leather sofas in the middle of the room. After they sat in silence for a while, he stood up again, apparently having made up his mind, and whispered: "To hell with it, I need one of those too."

"It seems you did well for yourself," Lenny said, looking up back and forth at the various pieces of furniture. A large coffee table, ostensibly designed to resemble the desk but also clearly of a different century, lay between the two sofas and their matching chairs. Interspersed at irregular intervals, floor-to-ceiling bookshelves indented inside the walls harboured more tomes and collected works he figured Charlie would have found the time to read. But, of course, he couldn't possibly know that.

"How did you know it was me?" Charlie asked after sitting down again.

Although he'd rehearsed this story a half-dozen times already, so well in fact that it flashed all at once in his mind's eye, the very last thing Lenny wanted to do right then was start making-up for lost time with a lie. Maybe there was a chance to steer him away from... from his palace? From his den of influence and power over millions of people? From his decadent life of crime? Maybe, but likely not today. Today's task was sipping scotch before noon and making sure Charlie didn't slam the button on his desk that would launch nukes to the four corners of the globe. Was there a button? Lenny glanced furtively.

"I started looking for you four or five years ago, figured you'd be all grown up and established and what not... I know this is going to sound pretty silly right now..." – he looked around with his classic half-frowning half-smiling face that he usually complemented with a 'womp womp' sound effect in his head – "but the reason I left you at that school was to make sure you didn't turn out like me. I didn't want you to grow up thinking the only way to get what you want in life is to take it away from others. So anyway, I was up in New England a few years back and stopped at the school, to ask them if they knew where to find you. They didn't. I was disappointed but, on the other hand, I'm not quite sure what I was expecting either, so… I was just about to leave and ran into one of your old teachers, Father Mallory I think it was…"

Charlie started slowly nodding up and down.

"He gave me just one look and said, 'Now here's a ghost from the past, yar Charlie Watson's dad, aren't ya.' Guess we kinda do look alike…" – Lenny smiled, Charlie remained stone faced – "anyway, he didn't give a guilt trip and we sat down for a few minutes. He filled me in best he could, told me how you asked to stay with them and how they convinced the State one of them could become your guardian. He told me you were by far the smartest young boy he'd ever met in his life, and that made me so proud and so sad at the same time. And just before I had to take off, he said he had a hunch about where you were. He said he recalled a conversation the two of you had when you were still just a kid, said he'd never forget it because he'd been scared a bit that you were so young and so smart, and you told him that someday you'd make sure nobody would be able to threaten life on Earth with things like pollution or nuclear war or that kind of thing. And when he asked you how you would do that, according to him, you said 'That's simple, I'll become Master of the World and get rid of the bad guys.'"

Charlie started laughing. "I did say that, now, didn't I? Poor, old Father Mallory, of course he knew I meant that."

"So anyway, he never said he thought you were… that this Balzac fella was you, not explicitly at least. But I got the hint and put it in my coat pocket and went back to doing what I do. I didn't really believe it at first, it was just a crazy thought, you know, a good anecdote for my memoirs kind of thing. But then all the other avenues I checked, they were all dead ends. I couldn't find a single trace of you anywhere I looked. So I started thinking this may be worth checking out, just in case, the odd chance..."

"So you hopped on a plane and came knocking at the door of South America's most powerful man on the odd chance he was the son you turned your back on 30 years ago? A man the United Nations designated as a dangerous terrorist?" He raised his glass to Lenny. "That was very bold of you."

"It took about a year to convince myself I needed to do this. I figured the worst that could happen was... you'd be someone else and maybe I'd look a bit foolish but–"

"– I disagree. A lot of very bad things could have happened to you. This is not Disneyworld."

Lenny chuckled. "That's what Flores said." He briefly toyed with the idea of letting him know Flores also referred to him as Mickey Mouse but decided to go in a different direction. "How much do you trust him?"

Charlie appeared taken aback. "Octavio? Why the sudden concern for my welfare?"

"Charlie, that's not fair."

"Isn't it?"

"I told you, I was afraid you'd turn up like me."

They were both silent for a moment.

"Yet, oddly, here we are," Charlie concluded. "It all rather sounds like a Greek tragedy, wouldn't you say? A dead mother, a well-intentioned father left his son to his own devices while attempting to escape a pre-determined fate, a course of action which unintentionally leads our protagonists back into the very situation they had meant to avoid. You couldn't have played it better."

"I never meant for any of this to happen," Lenny whispered, staring at the bottom of his tumbler.

"Cheer up, old man," Charlie said contentedly. "It's not all bad. Like I told Father Mallory, I am going to conquer the world. This would not have happened if you'd kept me on the travelling show with you. I wouldn't have received the world-class education I did, wouldn't have acquired the work ethic I did." Again, he raised his glass to Lenny. "Here's to your inevitable role in the march of progress."

"Do you have to? Conquer the world, I mean."

Charlie sat straight in his seat and frowned. "Oh, please tell me you didn't come here to try to save me from my wicked ways."

"No," Lenny protested. "Not entirely. Maybe." And suddenly, like a rabbit jumping out of the hat before the magician could pull it out, he'd chosen his side – family! –and realised he needed to level with his son. "Charlie, they're going to put you away, Uncle Sam and his friends! You can't think you're getting away with this."

Charlie sported a mischievous smile, like he couldn't believe what he had just heard, as he stood up and walked slowly towards the desk. "You mean they'll get to me just like they got to you?"

"It's not like that!" Lenny stood up and started to follow Charlie but caught himself and stopped in his tracks. "Sure, they squeezed me, but it doesn't need to end with them putting you away. It's like you just said: maybe *that* needed to happen for... for *this* to happen. It was inevitable." *I got you a flask*, he thought to himself. "We can still disappear, just you and me, just like when you were a kid–"

"–Ugh, stop it, will you! I hate to be the bearer of bad news, *Dad*, but *the good old days have gone away and they ain't comin' back no more.* You are too late and I have plans… Hell, I have a world to conquer, didn't you hear?"

"No!" Lenny said with as much fatherly authority as he could summon.

"Excuse me?"

"You heard what I said. This ends here and now. You and I are going to slip away from this place and go fishing in Mexico for a week. I know the perfect spot. It will do miracles for your mental state and nobody will have to be worried about you launching those nukes…"

Charlie's eyes widened to the size of silver dollars and he started laughing hysterically. Lenny wasn't having any of it.

"You think this is funny? Who the frigg raised you that you turned out to be so disrespectful of your father?"

"I'm sorry," Charlie was trying to say between fits of laughter. "I'm not laughing at you… it's what you said."

"What did I say?"

"The nukes… Is that what the CIA thinks is happening here? They think I'm depressed and I'm going to obliterate whoever looks at me the wrong way? Is that what they're worried about?"

"Aren't you?" Lenny asked sheepishly.

"Hold that thought, will you?" Charlie replied, still giggling, and walked over to the desk. He pushed a button and, speaking to some piece of unseen gadgetry, summoned Luis to come and join them. "Sit down, have another drink. This is too funny!" he then told Lenny.

The lock mechanism was released almost immediately. Luis must have been waiting outside this whole time, which prompted Lenny to wonder whether the study was completely soundproof. How much had Luis heard of their conversation? He'd just folded like a cheap polyester suit strewn in a duffle bag. They'd been wrong to entrust him with this mission. Leonard

Watson, saviour of humanity? Give me a break! They'd been wrong and he had told them so. This failure was egg salad on *their* face, not his! And one more thing these friggin' amateurs had been wrong about? Charlie was clearly not depressed. Sure, the man had some issues and sounded like he could use an hour or two in a Thai massage parlour, but depressed he was not. Another typical intelligence failure? More likely a bad case of broken telephone.

Luis walked in with a spring in his step, clipboard in his left hand. "How can I be of service, sir?"

Charlie pulled opened a drawer and reached inside. "Luis, I am so fucking disappointed in you."

Holding a pistol, he raised his arm and shot twice. Bullets caught Luis in the throat and forehead before he had time to say anything or react otherwise. Lenny dropped his tumbler and ducked behind a sofa as the sound of empty shell casings hitting the hard floor echoed inside his head.

Friggin' Christ Almighty, welcome to the Reunion from Hell!

"It's okay, Dad. You can come out," Charlie said.

"No way! You're going to have to come over here and hunt me down, you sick maniac!"

"No really, I'm not going to shoot you. Here, I'm putting the gun down."

Lenny heard the sound of metal being gently dropped on the desk. He peeked over the horizon of the sofa and saw Charlie holding both hands up on each side of his head, showing off empty palms.

"I'm not going to shoot you," Charlie repeated.

Lenny looked over to the other side of the room. Luis was lying face-up in a slowly expanding pool of his own blood. Poor kid! He wondered whether Duchaine and Purnell would ever know his name.

"Are you mad? You just killed him!" Lenny screamed, uncertain if anger or fear was fueling him at this very moment. "See, that's exactly what they were talking about, except with nukes!"

"Enough with that nonsense, nobody is going to get nuked."

"Why did you kill him?"

"He was a traitor."

Lenny fought the urge to throw up. "You don't know that," he said softly.

"In fact, I do," Charlie replied. "You're all the confirmation I needed."

"Me? Just because I said I got squeezed doesn't mean Luis had anything to do with it."

Charlie grabbed his tumbler and headed towards the bar. "Let me get you another one of those." He started filling another tumbler with a couple fingers of Glenfiddich when Lenny erupted.

"I don't need another drink! There is a dead man on the floor! You just shot him in the head!"

"I know what I did. Now sit down."

Lenny didn't know what to do. He glanced back and forth a few times between the dead man lying on the floor and the one handing him a tumbler of his favourite whiskey, and decided that yes, he needed to sit down.

"Don't worry, he's not going anywhere," Charlie reassured him. "I'm sorry for bringing you in the middle of this whole mess–"

"–You didn't bring me here."

"In a way, I did. I know this may be a bit confusing, but I had suspected for a while now there was a snitch within my ranks. Probably someone close. I figured they were reporting to the CIA or MI-6 or maybe even the

SVR. So I laid out a trap."

Lenny didn't quite follow yet. "I was a trap?"

"Actually you were *part* of an *elaborate* trap, to be more precise. You see, I started acting out, leaving clues here and there suggesting I may have been sinking into a distressed state of mind. I also confided into various associates about specific desires I thought might help me get back on my feet. I told Flores I was thinking of getting married. I also told my nurse, la senora Fernandez, I was thinking of getting married, but I needed to twist that one around, so my confession included a so-called coming out of the closet. And Luis, sadly the closest of my collaborators, was told my dearest wish was to reunite with my long-estranged father."

"So you weren't really looking for me?"

"Only as a way to root out the mole." Charlie hesitated. "But I also hoped it would be you. I don't really need a wife – or a husband, for that matter – but I'm glad you'll be around to witness my great achievement."

"You mean, when you take over the world?" Lenny snapped.

"Yes! Yes I do! Stop shitting all over it like I'm some kind of common thug, will you! This is important, at least a tad more than selling people timeshares located in the middle of a corn field!"

There it was, his legacy reduced to its bare essentials by the son he had abandoned in order to pursue it. He looked down, found his tumbler, and took a sip in silence. What else could he do but finish his drink and go home with his tail between his legs?

"Why is it important?" he asked. "Why does it have to be you?"

Charlie stood up again and started scanning the bookshelves. "Have you ever heard of the Fermi Paradox?" he asked but did not wait for – or expect – an answer. "Well, it concerns itself with the size and the age of the universe and the probability of life emerging in the four corners of the galaxy. After you boil it up and drain the fat, what you are left with, really, is a simple question: Where the hell is everyone?"

"What do you mean, like aliens?"

"I mean *Life* with a capital 'L', organic, sentient, driven by purpose to expand and perfect itself. The universe is 13.8 billion years old. If no other form of life has made contact with us yet, it stands to reason that we are alone."

"What does this have to do with you?"

"This is exactly why I'm needed," Charlie argued. "The probability of life emerging anywhere and everywhere is so overwhelming that it makes the notion of us being alone inconceivable. Admittedly, that's why it's a paradox but it begs to be resolved."

"So this is where you come in?"

Charlie turned towards him and smiled. "I know, you already think I'm halfway to the madhouse." He sighed and let his shoulders sag, unable to find the book he was looking for.

"They put me away in Alabama for much less than that," Lenny said and returned the smile. He thought Charlie started to sound just like him on a good day of work.

"Well," Charlie continued, "the most likely explanation for the Fermi Paradox is the existence of a common existential threat, like some kind of filter if you prefer, which life has to get through in order to achieve greatness and, eventually, scatter amongst the stars. The reason no other form of life has come to visit – or conquer us, for that matter – is none of them has managed to make it through the filter. And now it's our turn. I don't know what the filter is, it could be pollution, pandemic, nuclear war

– hell, it could simply be that it's the nature of intelligent life to destroy itself – but I do know that I don't trust any of the morons in charge out there to get us through. What if we're it? What if we're life's last-ditch experiment and we fail just like everyone else before us? We have a duty to carry on, and yes, that's why I have to conquer the world and make sure we don't fuck up!"

Lenny was positively dumbfounded. *This can't be true...* he thought... *the friggin' cyborg is still screwing through my brain and none of this is real!* "You're insane," he told Charlie. "You're pulling my leg. This is all a big farce, you put this all together to punk me or something. The DHS, the cyborg..." He half-expected Luis to stand up and start clapping, or Flores to come out from under the desk all smiling and pointing finger guns at him like he was saying 'You the Man.'

"I've never been more serious in my life," Charlie replied.

"I can't let you do this."

"What makes you think this is up to you? I spent my whole life planning for this moment. You show up 20 minutes before I'm ready to launch and you think you're going to shut me down? Not a chance!" Charlie walked over to the desk and flipped open a laptop computer. He typed in a short command, then looked up at Lenny and tapped the ENTER key with his index. "Done."

Lenny took an involuntary step back. "What? You launched World War Three just like that?"

"You didn't understand a thing I said, did you? That's the point. There will be no more war, no more bungled pandemic management, no more Chinese kids who think the colour of the sky is grey. I'm in charge now... or at least I will be in about ten days."

"Why, what happens in ten days?"

"That is when our friend the good Dr. Sereno will infiltrate and subjugate the military central command systems of the major powers."

"Dr. Sereno? But he's dead," Lenny objected.

"Who told you this, Luis?" Charlie glanced at the corpse. "Well, Luis was right, but only from a certain point of view. The notion that consciousness and intelligence need to be carbon-based is ridiculous and counterproductive. Dr. Sereno was in fact the first of us to become immortal... a minute ago."

That must have been what the cyborg meant. "The mind upload..." Lenny whispered.

"Yes, the mind upload. Dear God, Dad, you do know an awful lot about my business. I'll need to have a word with Flores."

"Spare the man, I ran into Lucas Montes on my way here," Lenny thought he should clarify.

"I see. Well, that's unfortunate. Lucas Montes is an abomination, even Felipe could see as much before he died. Did he get anything out of you?"

"He got everything I had."

"He probed your mind," Charlie guessed.

"Yes. And then one of your men killed him." He chose to hide the fact Montes' own memories had somehow melted into his. After today's revelations, this was something he would definitely take to his grave.

"Good. But it doesn't matter anymore. Whatever's left of the *Filhos do Filosofo* will be quickly rounded up once Dr. Sereno unleashes the power at his disposal. Hmm... filthy terrorists taken down by the AI incarnation of their spiritual father, who ever said there is no poetry in science?"

The computer emitted a quick but strident chime. Charlie perked up, visibly confused, and pivoted the device so he could examine the screen.

"Is everything alright?" Lenny asked him.

"He's ready…" Charlie whispered to himself. "How can that be?"

"What are you talking about?"

"Dr. Sereno… We had estimated he would require about ten days to absorb all the information available out there, everything that's online, everything stored in our own internal databases, and assimilate it all into a coherent strategy that would allow me to control the globe from this room. Instead, it took him all of two minutes."

"Is that good?" Lenny asked.

The computer chimed again. Charlie frowned.

"No, no no no! We're not ready for this yet, Felipe." He started typing frenetically. "Stay within your programming, you old kook!"

More chimes resonated, each sending a chill up Lenny's spine as Charlie's face contorted from looking apprehensive to troubled, and a few seconds later to distraught.

"How bad is it?" Lenny asked again.

"He's launching a massive cyber-attack against critical infrastructures in eastern Russia."

"Is that part of the plan?"

"Yes… yes, it is but… not so soon. Not now!" Charlie was still typing. "He's supposed to… oh damn! He knows."

"He knows what?"

Charlie stepped away from the keyboard.

"He knows what, Charlie?" Lenny insisted.

"He knows that I killed him."

Of course you did, you muddafrigger! 'Cause that's the way you roll, just ask poor Luis.

"So... you killed the guy and then gave him the capability to control every computer in the world, and you didn't think this could backfire on you?"

Charlie didn't look amused. "I didn't have a choice. I figured his mind was the only one that would recognise what had happened and would be able to adapt to the digital environment. Anyone else would have gone completely insane."

"Can you take him offline?"

"I can try but he's likely had enough time to build and hide redundant copies of himself all over the Net. I'd need an army of techies and it would turn out to be like a never-ending game of whack-a-mole."

Lenny reckoned he should call Agent Purnell. Surely the CIA and the NSA could figure this one out. Then he remembered how he was to contact them and glanced behind him. His asset was lying on the floor with a bullet hole in his forehead. Two steps ahead of him, his son – the criminal mastermind who, it would appear, had just handed over the fate of the world to a brain in a jar – was staring at the computer screen with idle hands fidgeting on each side of the keyboard. Yes, Charlie may've frigged up in ways unprecedented but at least, Lenny reckoned, he wasn't running away... like someone else he knew. "What's going to happen next," he asked, wishing there was something – anything – he could do to help.

"Well, Russia is the most volatile player, so he's going to take them out first. China and North Korea will be next, then the NATO countries, India and Pakistan, the Middle-east. This will hurt us for a while but..."—Lenny saw a spark in his eyes – "if I know him as well as I think I do, he's going to be dumb enough and set-up regional proxies to increase efficiency. And since it will be some time before he can replicate mind emulation, these will be simple AI machines – that's where we'll strike. We'll also need allies in odd places. I know some people but, Dad, I could use a front man who can sell anything to anyone…"

ABOUT THE EDITOR

JULIA T. LYE is a graduate of Carleton University living in Ottawa as she pursues a career in creative writing. Her short stories have been published in the horror anthology 'What Lies in Wait', the science fiction anthology 'The Stranger Side of Tomorrow', and the romance anthology 'You Hit Me with Your Car (and Other Love Stories)', and her debut novel, 'Anelisha Knight in the Yarns of Gods', was published by DeeBee Books in May of 2019. When she isn't tapping away at her keyboard, she likes to run original Dungeons and Dragons campaigns, read any book she can get her hands on, and create digital art. You can reach her at lyejulia@gmail.com or check out her website at www.julialye.com

ACKNOWLEDGMENTS

This collection of short stories would not have been possible without the energy and enthusiasm of the Ottawa Workshop writers who contributed their talents to it. These stories emerged from the Fall 2019 Science Fiction and Fantasy workshop held in Ottawa.

Thanks for reading! If you enjoyed this collection, please add a short review on Amazon and/or Goodreads.

Reviews mean a lot to writers, so I encourage you to support our growing writers' community by taking a few minutes now to rate this collection and write a few words of encouragement about it. And please share your copy of the book with others!

www.ingramcontent.com/pod-product-compliance
Lightning Source LLC
Chambersburg PA
CBHW032013170626
46807CB00006B/2789